YOU'LL BE MINE

A HEARTS BEND NOVEL

RACHEL HAUCK

MANDY BOERMA

sunrise
PUBLISHING

PRAISE FOR THE HEARTS BEND COLLECTION

You'll Be Mine is a delightful opportunity to revisit the fictional town of Hearts Bend, TN, created by bestselling author Rachel Hauck. Debut author Mandy Boerma teams with Hauck to create a perfect blend of romance, rediscovery, and reconciliation that kept me turning the pages and had me smiling with satisfaction as I reached the end of Cami and Ben's love story.

— BETH K. VOGT, CHRISTY AWARD-WINNING AUTHOR

You'll Be Mine is an adorably charming story of second chances, finding hope, and coming home again. Whether you're a first-time visitor or a return guest, you'll love your stay in Hearts Bend.

— LINDSAY HARREL, AUTHOR OF *THE INN AT WALKER BEACH*

A heart-warming romance, *One Fine Day* is a great way ̣end a day and tease your sweet tooth. Now I need ̣to my local bakery!

̣. LOWE, BESTSELLING AUTHOR OF *UNDER THE MAGNOLIAS*

One Fine Day reunites a determined pastry chef and a former pro athlete for a second chance at love. Settle in for a charming escape in this small-town romance that's sure to warm your heart!

— DENISE HUNTER, BESTSELLING AUTHOR OF THE RIVERBEND ROMANCE SERIES

A NOTE FROM RACHEL

Dear friends,

Welcome back again to Hearts Bend, Tennessee, where love and magic seem to happen.

Where a wedding chapel is the symbol of true love. Where a wedding shop comes back to life. Where a country superstar finds his one and only. Where the disgraced hometown girl finds her handsome prince...literally.

Where a widowed pastry chef finds love with a childhood friend, who went on to become a star NFL quarterback (*One Fine Day.*)

There is something comforting about returning to a favorite place in both novels and real life.

In Mandy Boerma's charming *You'll Be Mine*, Ben Carter (a prosperous hotelier) and Cami Jackson (a smart, successful property developer) find themselves in a tangle over the future of Hearts Bend Inn. Can their past affection for the old establishment impact their future?

I'm all in for second-chance romances as well as childhood-friends-to-grown-up-lover stories, so I found myself invested in Ben and Cami.

The reunited friends—well, we know they're sweet on each other— are surrounded by a fun and quirky cast of characters.

While the inn seems to be at the heart of her hero and heroine's conflict, you'll soon discover there are deeper issues in play. But with a bit of kindness, love and honesty, and a whisper from God, Ben and Cami might have the love story their hearts desire.

Mandy's quirky, chicklit voice is perfect for any romance, especially one set in Hearts Bend. I know you're going to enjoy her.

So dear reader, I present to you, *You'll Be Mine*, and the fabulous Mandy Boerma. Enjoy!

With affection,

Rachel Hauck

To Sam.
Thanks for dreaming with me.

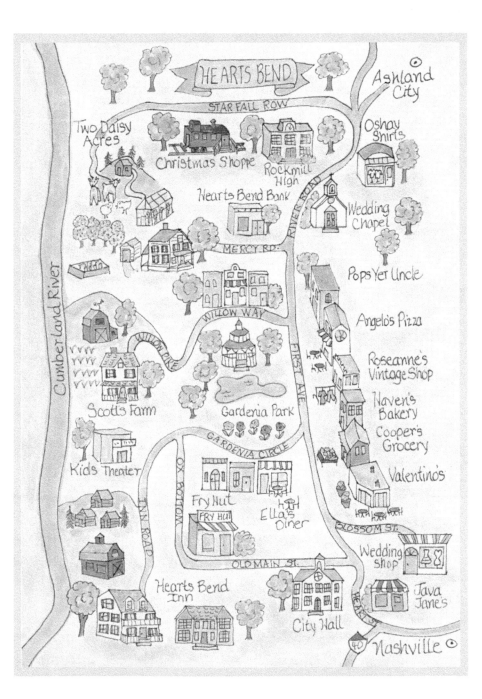

CHAPTER 1

*C*upcakes, coffee, and closing a huge deal, all before lunchtime. What more could a girl want?

New shoes? Absolutely.

The cherry red Prada pumps Cami wore today were her splash of color to close the deal with Emerson—the largest property Akron Development had acquired in the last two years, in Nashville, Tennessee, where the main office was located. All negotiated by Camellia Jackson, the boss's daughter, thank you very much, with zero, zip, nada help from him.

Cami exited the elevator on the second floor from the top to a round of applause.

"Way to go, Cami!"

"Chip off the ole block!"

"On fire, girl!"

A shrill whistle pierced the air, breaking through the symphony of office sounds—keyboards clicking, voices humming, and printers printing. Had to be Maddy Patterson, who coached her daughter's softball team. Yep, when Cami looked around, Maddy's fingers were on her lips, forming another loud whistle.

Cami bowed and curtsied. Was she glowing? She felt like she was. "Thank you all. I couldn't have done it without the amazing team here at Akron."

Maddy whistled again as Cami made her way to her office, soaking in all the attention. Make no mistake, she'd worked hard for this one. Really hard. Because being the boss's daughter afforded her nothing.

"Love the shoes! Jimmy?" This from Astrid, Cami's personal assistant, who stood by her office ready to trade Cami's Gucci purse and attaché for an iPad and a Perrier. Soothing jazz piped through a speaker hidden behind a silk plant in the corner. Astrid always played music, insisting she needed to cover the noise outside their office that filtered in when the door was open, which was always.

"Prada. And nothing says success like red shoes."

Cami's shoes were her *thing* outside of closing deals for her father's company. Which was her number one thing. She strived for his approval. Don't judge. At least she could admit it.

"I'd love to talk shoes and shopping, but..." Astrid said with a hesitation in her voice. "Brant wants to see you."

Cami stared at her assistant. "You're kidding." Dad, aka Brant, was always busy when she closed deals. It took days, sometimes weeks, for him to congratulate her on a deal.

While her colleagues had his approval, praise, and delight, atta boys, atta girls, slaps on the back, celebratory steak dinners, plaques for their walls, goofy trophies for their desks, Cami received a passing congratulations and eventually, sometimes, her steak dinner.

When it came to his dear ole daughter, Brant Jackson's

words were few. Sometimes she wondered if it pained him to really praise her.

"Not kidding. He buzzed down right before you came in," Astrid said.

Cami started for the door. "Do you know what it's about?"

"Haven't a clue."

The duo walked to the elevator together. Astrid whispered a *good luck* then turned back to their office space. Good luck? Why would she need it? She'd just closed a huge deal. Was he actually calling her up to his penthouse office to congratulate her?

Dad was sitting at his desk when Cami knocked lightly on his open office door. "You wanted to see me?"

"Cami," he said, standing. "Come in, come in."

For years now, her relationship with Dad had seemed to be a tug of war. Which one would show some sort of affection first? As a teen, Cami had felt it was her father's responsibility, especially after Mom died. But she'd learned quickly she would have to extend the olive branch. Which had eventually made her angry. Which had made her quit trying.

However, he knew she'd closed the Emerson deal, so was he finally bending first?

"I'm flying down to Palm Beach this afternoon." Dad moved to the chair at the small glass-top table in the corner of his office. "Roger Davis finally agreed to meet about his oceanfront property. I was going to take you for your steak dinner, but I'll need to reschedule."

She struggled to mask her surprise. He'd been going to take her to dinner? "I can't go tonight anyway. I made plans with Annalise." Her sister was her best friend and counselor.

When Dad had cancelled Cami's steak dinner after her second—or was it third?—big acquisition, Annalise had thrown her a surprise dinner. Her husband, Steve, had sizzled steaks on the grill along with corn on the cob. Annalise had made Mom's green bean casserole and homemade apple cake and invited half a dozen of their childhood friends. She and Steve were the picture-perfect, happily in love couple.

It'd been the best steak dinner ever. Cami smiled, remembering.

To Cami Jackson, Nashville's next great businesswoman.

In her seven years on the job, Cami had worked harder than anyone else to get to the top. And now, here she sat, in the boss's grand, top floor office.

"I had dinner with your sister and Steve last night," Dad said. "Look, we'll reschedule your congratulatory dinner." His fixed smile was part father, part boss.

She wanted to say she'd not hold her breath, but refrained. With Dad, Brant, it was always something. A golf game. Another business deal. Or just the general excuse of "too busy." He'd not solidified anything with her for tonight even though he'd known from the staff meetings and her emails, as well as her weekly report, she was closing the deal.

"So, Roger?" Cami said. "You finally wore him down. Congratulations." She shifted her stance, trying to get comfortable in Dad's stiff, formal office.

His expansive cherry desk sat in front of the floor-to-ceiling windows overlooking the Cumberland River, which was vastly different than her view that looked over the downtown Nashville streets. A small sitting area of black leather pieces sat in the far corner and were more aesthetically pleasing than functionally comfortable.

On the other side of the office was a glass and metal conference table with black leather chairs. The beige walls were, well...beige. And empty. Devoid of art and anything else of color.

If it weren't for the large pane windows overlooking the

river, the place would be a desert for any creative mind.

"We both knew he'd cave sooner or later." Dad pointed to a pink box from Sweet Tooth Bakery on the small table. He pulled out a chair and sat, gesturing for Cami to follow suit. "Jeremy ordered your congratulatory cupcakes." He smiled as if the treats were a perfectly suitable substitute for a celebratory steak dinner with the boss and founder of the company. "He asked for the chocolate ones you like."

"Thank you." Really, she'd have to remember to thank Dad's assistant on her way out. The cupcake tradition was usually for the staff meeting. This private celebration surprised and touched her.

Over the years, she'd adjusted to their cordial, non-affectionate father-daughter relationship, and it worked well for Akron Development. It was how things were between them since Mom died.

"Is that why you called me up here?" Cami opened the pink lid to reveal two double fudge chocolate cupcakes.

She pulled one out and reached for the napkins next to the box, then slid the box toward her dad.

Sun filtered through the windows, giving the dull office some brightness as Cami sank her teeth into the delectable treat. Calories didn't count on closing day. Especially with a multi-million-dollar property.

"I'm going ahead with the new office in Indianapolis." Dad took a small bite of his cupcake and returned it to the box before he reached for a napkin. "Indianapolis is too hot a market to delay any longer." His heavy, steady gaze landed on her. "I want you to head it up."

Cami stared at him, lip deep in chocolate cake and frosting. "Hmmphph?" She chewed with a napkin over her mouth, swallowing, trying not to choke. "What?"

"You're opening the Indy office." Dad moved to his desk to

retrieve a large green folder and brought it back to Cami and sat down again. "While you closed on your deal, I closed on office space. Here's the information. It's a blank slate, so you can build it out however you want. You'll find the name of a recommended contractor and the budget for the remodel. I want the work done and the office up and running by September first, so you've got a lot to do."

"Wait, wait, what?" September first? Less than three months away. "Dad, I thought we were not going to risk the capital right now."

"I looked at the data. We need to go now. I'm starting to feel we're already too late. Are you in? Because if you're not..." Dad reached for the folder. "I'll see if Geoffrey—"

She stopped his hand before he could take the folder. "Can you give me a second to wrap my head around this? You didn't think to at least ask me first?" She was on her feet. "I have a life here, you know." Not much of one, but he didn't need to know. "Friends, Annalise." Could she live four hours from her sister? "I just moved into my condo a few months ago. I finally got my soaker tub last week. I have a view of the river."

Her shoe closet was the size of a small bedroom, mostly because it *was* the spare bedroom. She'd spent months designing and decorating, picking the colors, the fixtures. She finally had *her home.*

"You can sell it for a profit. Downtown lofts are up fifteen percent." Was it always about numbers with him? "Or you can lease it if you want. But you're heading up Indy." Dad rose up, stretching to the six foot three that used to make her feel safe and protected.

"And if I refuse?" The emotion flowing through her made her voice quiver, and she resented it.

"Cami, you've been telling me for two years you want a pathway to promotion. You want to take on more responsibility.

You want to take over the company one day. Don't tell me you didn't mean it."

"I meant it." No doubt Indianapolis was the opportunity she needed to advance, so why did it feel like her father was sending her away?

From his desk, Dad's landline buzzed, and he circled around to answer it, giving Cami a moment to compose herself. After a five-word conversation with Jeremy, he returned to their little table of chocolate cupcakes and surprises.

But the short interlude gave her time to think, take her emotions in command. The city *was* ripe for expansion. It *was* a fantastic move for the company, and if she'd get her head on straight, a huge stepping-stone for her.

"What's it going to be, Cami? You can refuse, of course, or resign, but yes, Indy is yours. You'll be promoted to director. If things go well, vice president after two years." Dad leaned toward her. "This is what you wanted, isn't it?"

"Yes." Cami cleared her voice. "Yes, thank you, it is." When Dad retired, there would be no doubt in anyone's mind that she'd earned his office through her own merit. She could do this...spend a few years in Indy, then head back down to Nashville. "All right." She sat back in her chair and opened the green folder. "Give me the details."

Dad relaxed with an exhale and smiled. "I bought a refurbished warehouse in the center of the business district. Take what office space you need, then rent out the rest. Build out your space first, then oversee the rest. Give yourself two years to complete the build-out. But you, Cami, I'm serious, be ready by the first of September. Get Astrid to start posting jobs for the positions you want to fill. Make a list of potential Akron folks who might like to transfer up north."

Really? Who'd want to leave Nashville?

"You should talk to her about going with you." Dad peeked

into the pink box. "I think you'll need her." He considered the rest of the cupcakes, then closed the lid.

This was why he was so great in business, in life, in everything. Discipline. When they passed around cupcakes in the staff meeting or gathered for the quarterly office potluck, Brant Jackson proudly proclaimed he only weighed ten pounds more than in his high school wrestling days.

But when it came to Cami, his disciplined life, emotions went too far.

"Maybe," she said. "Astrid's been going on and on about Boyfriend proposing." He had a real name, which Cami couldn't recall at the moment. "I'm not sure she'll want to go."

"Hasn't she been dating him for a while?" Dad made a face. "If he's not proposed by now, he probably won't."

"Well, I'm not going to tell her that, Dad." With him, business always came first. Even over family. Over his wife and daughters. But if Astrid had a chance for a happily ever after, even with a sloth for a boyfriend, Cami wasn't going to stand in her way.

"Someone should. Get her to go with you, Cami. She's one of the best. If I didn't have Jeremy, I'd steal Astrid from you." Dad pointed to the folder again. "The real estate agent sent some apartments for you to review."

Cami flipped through the top pages, all apartment listings. Already she could tell they wouldn't compare to her beautiful downtown loft, the one she'd customized for herself.

She read the name on the real estate agent listing. Max Caldwell.

"I-I'll call today." September first would be here way too fast.

"Good. Glad you're on board, Cami." Dad stood, indicating the conversation was coming to a close. "I saw on the project board you're working the Landmark Shopping Complex.

Chatted with Jared Landry the other day, and he said you'd approached him about it. Excellent property, Cami, but I want you focused on the Indy office. You won't have time for a Landmark kind of deal."

Cami stood, reaching for the cupcake box. More than half of hers remained. But then she glanced at her lean father and changed her mind. "Dad, do you lecture Geoffrey or Mark on how to manage their lives *and* their jobs? Or just me?"

Dad regarded her with something she interpreted as respect. And she'd take it. "Good point. You've proven yourself. Do what you feel you must but, Cami, my advice is to focus on Indy."

He was right. Of course, he was the great Brant Jackson. Already, details of the massive project had started swirling in her head. She had a lot to do in two and a half months.

"Can I ask why September first?"

"The city gave us a huge tax break if we open by the third quarter. The contractor's bid goes to August thirtieth. He can finish the build-out, but if we don't get on it, give him enough time, he can't guarantee when he can complete the work. He has another job September first. That's why we have a two-year goal on opening the rest of the property."

"Then I have work to do." The sweetness of the cupcake soured as she walked toward the door. Then for some odd reason, she got a bit of *grr* in her gut and spun around. "You need artwork in here, Dad. Why don't you let me acquire some for you before I go?"

"That's not necessary, Cami."

"But it is necessary. How do you work in this uninspired space?"

Dad tapped his temple. "I've all I need in here."

She sighed, eyed the pink box one more time, then bid her father a good trip. "Tell Roger hi for me."

By the time she made it back to her office, her head was pounding with details, her red shoes pinched her toes, and she felt completely void of the cheering and accolades from thirty minutes ago.

Her head swirled with details as she descended down to her real world. Budgets, staff, properties, moving, selling or leasing, *moving*, Annalise, moving.

Did she want to move? Dad was her boss, but she was also a valued team member, and if she didn't want to move, she didn't have to move.

Don't kid yourself, Cami Jackson. If Dad asked her to move for the good of his company, which was her future, she'd do it. She ached for him to be proud of her. To level his laser gaze at her and call her daughter. She was twenty-nine years old and in so many ways, still a little girl.

Rounding the corner to her office, she bumped into Angie from accounting, who thrust a cell phone into her hand.

"Cami, I was just heading to your office. Liam and I are looking at artwork for our living room. We found this at an estate auction. We love it, but what do you think? Is it good? Is it worth the price?"

"Good for you and Liam." She should call her friend Marta, see what she thought about her loft. Sell or lease. She was one of Nashville's top Realtors. "Art, um, art always makes a space richer." Cami paused outside her office to focus on the small screen.

"Well, what do you think?" Angie said.

"It's beautiful." Art was Cami's other passion besides acquiring properties at rock-bottom prices then developing them just enough to sell at top prices. She'd minored in art appreciation at the University of Georgia because she loved it. But jobs in art appreciation were hard to come by.

When Dad had offered to "show her the ropes" at Akron, she'd jumped at the chance. Not because she loved numbers and spreadsheets or walking rundown properties and negotiating the best deal, but because she wanted to be near the man who seemed to hold her at arm's length.

Hadn't taken too long to discover she was a chip off the old block, which meant she didn't have time to pursue her own art anymore. She used her artistic skills in contract negotiations and seeing the potential of a property.

In the meantime, she helped friends like Angie pick out pieces for their homes and offices. Cami studied the picture, zooming in on simple lines, the contrasting colors, the dynamic scene. "It looks like a Briana Jones. Did they name the artist?"

Angie shook her head, her dark hair pinned up behind her ears and flowing in a straight curtain down her neck. "Is it good? I love it, but what do I know? Liam really wants to *invest* in a piece of art. Do you think this would be a good one?"

"Honestly, there's always a risk in buying artwork as an investment when you don't know the artist. But this picture is reminiscent of Briana Jones, a student of Georgia O'Keeffe who modeled her style with a modern twist. If it's one of hers it would be an incredible find. Ask the seller to look for a BJ somewhere in the scene. Briana likes to hide her signature. Often people don't know they have expensive artwork and let it go for pennies. Even if it isn't valuable, if you like it, it would be a good investment. Art is meant to be enjoyed."

"Thank you, Cami." Angie clutched her phone to her chest. "I'll ask, but I do love it. I'll tell Liam it's a Briana Jones, because I *really* want this." She laughed and winked at Cami, taking steps down the hallway. "I'll keep you posted."

Cami closed her office door, which meant *leave me be*, and

checked her email, but her heart more and more tangled in Dad's news.

You're heading up Indy.

All right. She'd do what she always did. Follow orders. Own the field. And if success in Indy got her promoted to veep, well, she was all in.

Cami opened the folder and reviewed the details, made notes, and started an email of to-dos for Astrid. She messaged Marta, who texted back right away.

Are you kidding? Really? Well, let me get to work.

Yes, get to work. It seemed the only way for Cami to wrap her heart around this sudden and jarring new direction.

Her phone pinged. Annalise. Reminding her they had a sister night.

Don't forget. Six o'clock. Don't be late. It's supposed to rain, and I want to be at the restaurant before it starts. Wear sensible shoes!

Cami laughed. One time she'd worn stilettos to a garden wedding and spent the entire evening aerating the soil with her heels.

But once a big sister, always a big sister. After their mom had died, Annalise, who was five years older, had owned the mother role. She'd even moved home while she finished college just to be around for Cami during her final high school years. No amount of reminders that Cami was all grown up now, a college graduate and successful businesswoman, would change anything for Annalise. And Cami loved her for it.

Cami responded, promising to be on time, then went back to her email. A new one had just dropped in from Keith Niven, the Hearts Bend Realtor who kept in touch with Akron folk about properties in the small, quaint town of Hearts Bend northwest of Nashville.

Cami clicked on the email. *What are you up to, Keith?*

She liked the gregarious Realtor. Perhaps he had ambitions outside of his small town. With his good looks and energy, he'd be a good addition to Akron. It was a wonder Dad hadn't recruited him. A few years ago he'd worked hard to get Dad the property on Blossom. The old Wedding Shop. But the historical society had stepped in and ended their journey.

She jotted down his name as a potential for the Indy office, then skimmed Keith's email.

She'd couldn't imagine wanting anything in Hearts Bend, the town where her heart had literally, suddenly, in one afternoon, bent until it was completely broken. She'd not been back in fifteen years.

Unique property...interested in...Hearts Bend Inn.

Cami fired to her feet, nearly toppling her chair. The Hearts Bend Inn was for sale? She read the email in earnest.

There's a unique property potentially coming on the market you may be interested in. Mrs. Carter died. It's rumored the Hearts Bend Inn will go up for sale. I thought I'd reach out. You mentioned to me once you had fond memories there. It's not the multimillion-dollar property you usually acquire, but I thought you might want to take a look.

There it was. A little tug, the feeling of belonging. Of home. For a moment, the urge to return to the inn overpowered her. She wrestled with the sentiment but couldn't completely stop the whispers over her heart.

She hadn't been back to the inn since she was a scared, grieving fifteen-year-old. She wasn't sure she wanted to return now as a strong, confident almost-thirty-year-old. There were too many memories, too many buried emotions. In many ways, she wanted to forget. In others, she wanted to leave her past resting, at peace, the images, and feelings undisturbed by time.

Still, with Indy looming on her horizon, maybe a final goodbye to Hearts Bend and the inn, Mom's favorite place on earth, would do her good. The place might be sold to someone else in the next year.

Change was imminent.

Dad had warned her to stay focused, but there was nothing in Hearts Bend to distract her. Nothing to keep her from proving she was ready and able to take over his company.

CHAPTER 2

*T*he last hotel on earth Ben Carter wanted to run was his grandparents' country inn with its dark basement of steep stairs and mountain of boxes.

The stairs from the basement of Hearts Bend Inn to the small private office space Granddaddy and Granny had used for the last sixty years seemed to grow steeper with each load of boxes Ben carried up.

Granny had decades' worth of boxes in the basement. Had Granddaddy known she never threw anything away? Yesterday, Ben had thrown away guestbooks from the 1950s, '60s, and '70s. Granny had taken over full management of the inn when Granddaddy had grown too sick. Her organization skills had been, well, lacking. She'd kept everything—bills, letters, receipts. Even the weekly flyers from the grocery store. Like anyone needed to know the price of milk five years ago.

But if he could, Ben would happily talk to Granny about the price of milk, or anything she wanted, just to see her face again.

He'd been so busy the last five years, launching new and

marquee hotels for the prestigious Viridian Jewel Resorts around the world, that he'd not come home enough. He'd not helped out. Which in his mind made him a bad grandson. Especially after all his grandparents had done for him.

He set the box down next to the old desk. He could still see Granddaddy sitting here in the solo light of the lamp, balancing the books.

He should have been here for Granny. Should have seen that she needed help before and after Granddaddy passed. They'd run the inn together for sixty-one years, so he'd figured she didn't need him. Never mind she kept telling him everything was fine. *Go on and live your life, Benji. Open those big, beautiful luxury hotels.*

He'd believed her because he'd wanted to believe her.

Grabbing a handful of old tax returns from the box, he fed the paper shredder. As the machine hummed, he stared out the window toward the vegetable and herb garden on the east side of the inn. Sunlight streamed in, brightening up the whole room. Even if this place was a mess, at least it was a cozy mess with plenty of light.

The shredding work was mindless, but it gave him time to consider what else needed to be done. He'd been compiling an extensive to-do list since he arrived two weeks ago.

He only had the summer to get things settled, make decisions before he had to be in Sydney. The Emerald, a stunning world-class resort and the newest hotel for VJR, would be their marquee property in the South Pacific. This hotel would open up Asia to them, and Ben was heading the team. It had to go well. He was lucky his boss had let him come home to square up the estate.

But he must be back in Australia by September first. The last month was critical. As it was, he spent his evenings answering emails and texts from his boss and the team.

He fed another pack of papers through the shredder. He was exhausted.

Mr. Graham, Granny's lawyer, was stopping in today. He'd insisted on coming to the inn for coffee and cookies and for what Ben suspected to be bad news.

His phone vibrated in his back pocket. Jordan, his second-in-command in Sydney, had texted a picture. It was the promotional angle of the fifteen-story building. The lights inside glowed against the dark sky, the huge white domes of the Sydney Opera House lit up in the background. *Perfect.* Things were coming together, which eased a bit of his stress.

The inspector was set to give them the CO in a few weeks, and if possible, he wanted to be there. Setting up the lobby, the kitchen, the dining hall, the rooms, the spa required a lot of time and attention to detail.

If everything went well, and it would, Hong Kong was next. Investors were already lined up.

Thanks to his grandparents, the hotel business was in his blood. All his years at the Hearts Bend Inn checking in customers, waiting tables in the small dining room, mopping the kitchen, cleaning rooms, changing bed sheets, and fixing plumbing with Granddaddy looking over his shoulder had set him up for his career with Viridian.

The Emerald would solidify his career. He would not, *could not* fail. The irony of dealing with details for the Emerald while standing in his grandparents' old-fashioned place in the middle of Podunk, Tennessee, was not lost on him.

His phone pinged with another text from Jordan.

Don't forget we have a video call with the Hong Kong investors next week.

As if he could forget. The call fell right in the middle of the night for him, but he'd be up and dressed to impress.

It's on my calendar.

17

The quicker he figured out what to do with this inn, the quicker he could return to his life. His calling. To Sydney.

He finished the shredding and broke down the empty box. When he tossed the cardboard toward the pile against the wall, he managed to knock a frame off the desk.

Sorry, Granny.

Ben retrieved the old frame and set the picture in its spot of honor. The loving couple beneath the glass were a snapshot of love, of a blissful marriage, of home. Granddaddy, in his Army uniform, hugging Granny outside the inn. Happiness, love, commitment—all written across their faces.

Granddaddy had left his mark on the world as a decorated Korean War vet and retired from the Army after twenty years. He'd been a loved and respected citizen of Hearts Bend and the hero of Ben's life.

Ben gathered the tipping stack of cardboard and carried it to the dumpster hidden behind a fence and stand of trees. As he returned to his office, he paused just outside the kitchen doors and peered into the inn's lobby and dining area.

It was a beautiful place, sweet and charming, cozy in all the right ways. Granny had done the best she could keeping up the general appearance of the inn, but Ben knew, sure as he breathed, the bones beneath were brittle and in need of repair.

In the lobby, the cherry antique reception desk sat on the far wall facing the front door. And it was empty. As was the huge dog bed behind the desk. His great-aunt, Myrtle May, Granny's sister, was supposed to be there answering the phone, checking email for reservations. But she was nowhere in sight.

"Myrtle May?" Ben glanced down the hall, then to the front porch. How many times had he reminded Aunt Myrtle May to not leave the front desk vacant?

Maybe it was his high-end hotel training, but it made sense

to always have someone at the front desk, ready to take reservations and greet the guests.

No wonder business was slow.

Meanwhile, the warm aroma of sweet cinnamon and sugar filled the inn. Walt's cookies. Best in the world—at least Ben thought so. But don't tell that to any of the pastry chefs he'd worked with around the world. Or to Haven's Bakery just down the road.

The inn offered lunch and those amazing cookies all afternoon, along with sweet tea, hot tea, and coffee. Which was a sad shame, because Walt's coffee had to be the worst tasting cup of mud in the state. Note to self: find a new coffee source.

The grandfather clock next to the piano on the opposite wall chimed the top of the hour. Eleven gongs echoed through the lobby. The lawyer would be here any minute.

Since Myrtle May was out, Ben slid behind the desk and pulled up the reservations. At Ben's recommendation, Granddaddy had installed an online system, despite Granny's protests, and insisted everyone, even Walt, learn to use it.

Myrtle May had the calendar open showing only a handful of reservations, which explained the bank balance. With so few bookings, it was a wonder the inn survived. Since the inn was in a trust and Ben was now the owner, he had to pay all the bills after Granny's funeral.

Maybe he needed to just haul all the boxes to an incinerator and get on with the finances of the inn.

The bell over the front door jingled, and Lawrence Graham, Granny's attorney, was ushered in with a strong gust of wind. The sunshine from ten minutes ago had disappeared behind an angry cloud.

His warm dark eyes caught Ben's as he adjusted his suit and tie while he approached the reservations desk. "Weatherman says we're in for a real doozy tonight. Best tighten down the hatches. How're you doing, Ben?"

"Exhausted, if I'm honest. I hope you have good news for me." Coming around the desk, Ben shook the older man's hand.

Mr. Graham had been his grandparents' lawyer since Ben could remember. He was tall, dark-skinned, smart, and looked almost the same as he had twenty years ago, only with a graying head of hair.

"Good news? Not so sure, but I've plenty of good advice." He pointed toward the western windows. "Best check that big oak right outside. It's bending in this wind, and I'm sure it's rotten. Told your Granny five years ago to get rid of it, but she refused. Said her Benji used to climb that tree."

"I did. Granddaddy and I built a tree house in it," Ben said, moving to the window. The tree stood tall, swaying in the gusty breeze, looking steady and strong. He had practically lived in that tree after his parents left him with his grandparents the summer they returned to Papua New Guinea to serve with the Pacific Isle Mission. "I had my first kiss in that tree house. Cami Jackson."

"Did you, now?" Mr. Graham's chuckle was full of sentiment.

She'd been cute, fun, and destined to be a great artist. She would come from Nashville with her mother and sit in the shade of the inn's cottages with her easel and paints. In fact, Cami's mom had painted the large picture behind the desk. Granny had always said she was just holding it for the family.

One day they'll come for it.

"We were in the tree when we suddenly heard this loud crack. Next thing you know, we're falling to the ground, arms and legs flailing."

Man, had that been fifteen years ago already?

Mr. Graham chuckled. "Did she ever speak to you again?"

"She did, believe it or not. Until her mom passed and she stopped visiting the inn."

"Sentiment aside, my boy"—Mr. Graham headed for the coffee station—"best take that tree down before it goes down and does some damage."

He made quick work at the coffee station, pouring a cup of Walt's coffee. Did Ben apologize now or wait until Mr. Graham pumped his fist against his burning chest?

"Walt's coffee is in a class all its own." Mr. Graham took a long swallow. "How are you settling into Hearts Bend and the inn, Ben?"

"Granny was a pack rat." Ben led the lawyer to the office.

"I told her to get rid of all that stuff too, but it made her feel connected to your grandfather. Can't say as I blame her." Mr. Graham eased down into the chair opposite the desk.

"Your parents well? Still missionaries?"

Ben took his seat behind the desk with a passing glance at his grandparents' picture. "Yes, in Papua New Guinea. It's home to them." Just like the inn was home to him. "Thirty-five years in the field."

"What about you?" Mr. Graham said. "Where's home? I think your Granny was hoping the inn would be home for you."

Had she told him that or was he surmising? Granny had never said anything to Ben but to chase his dreams.

"Mr. Graham, I have a job that I love." Ben shifted forward, resting his hands on the old desk. "I have to be in Sydney by September first to open a marquee hotel for Viridian Jewel Resorts. The success of their South Pacific expansion begins with the success of the Sydney hotel."

Mr. Graham blew a low whistle. "That's quite an achievement. Well done. I suppose a place like that is very different from this tiny little inn." Mr. Graham set his coffee on the edge of the desk and opened his briefcase. "Where you got your start."

What was that supposed to mean? Ben studied the older African American who'd been a confidant and friend to his grandparents, especially Granny after Granddaddy died. He trusted him to be his friend and confidant as well. And he had warned Ben about the tree.

But Ben didn't need a reminder of where he'd come from or where he'd gotten his start.

"I'll get right to it," Mr. Graham said. "Your grandparents took out a loan."

"A loan?" Ben reached for the folder Mr. Graham offered. "I've paid bills and looked through the finances. I didn't see a loan." When he'd moved Granddaddy to the reservation system, he'd also brought the billing and accounting online. A loan would've been in the database.

"Vern and Jean Carter took out a loan with Stan down at Hearts Bend Bank when all the plumbing had to be redone a while back. They remodeled the bathrooms while they were at it and updated the owner's home." Mr. Graham pointed at the folder. "It's all in here."

Ben flipped through the papers, found the loan. Two hundred thousand dollars. And noticed the date. "Eight years ago?" He looked up at the lawyer. "How has the loan not been paid off?"

"You know how your granny was after your granddaddy died. Grieving, lost. She'd start to do the books, which was never her forte, get up for a cup of coffee, and next thing you know, six days had passed and she'd forgotten all about it."

"How did she pay any bills?"

"You know folks around here...they'd come by, tell her what was owed, and she'd apologize profusely and write the check."

"How did she know how much money she had?"

"Stan told her. Every once in a while, he'd have her pay on the loan, keep the interest at bay. Stan gave her extension after extension, but in the end there was nothing he could do about the interest adding up." Mr. Graham sipped his coffee and motioned for Ben to keep looking at the papers. "Jean didn't pay anything for two years. The bank is more or less calling the loan. Everything is to be paid by September first."

All the light in the room faded. "Two hundred grand by September?"

"'Fraid so, son. The inn and all her possessions are part of the trust, which you are now the head of. If Jean just flat-out had a will and died, the loan would be forgiven, but the trust borrowed the money. In simple terms—"

"The debt is mine."

"The bank was very lenient with Jean. They served her with a foreclosure notice, but when her health turned, Stan refused to pursue dollars and cents when the sweet woman was on her deathbed."

On her deathbed. The words painted a picture Ben had never considered. He knew his parents had flown home to be with her, but no one, no one had said anything to him.

"When she went on to glory last month, Stan wanted to give you a few weeks to get settled. But Hearts Bend Bank is now under a big corporate entity, and the higher-ups are putting pressure on them to clean up all their neighborly loans. He has no choice." His thick Southern drawl filled with sympathy.

Tums—he needed Tums. Opening the center drawer of the desk, Ben grabbed the antacids and popped a couple in his mouth.

He dropped the folder to the desk and moved to the window. Dark clouds collected in the blue sky, and a strong wind batted around the tree branches.

"You could sell," Mr. Graham said. "Keith Niven tells me the market for this sort of establishment is ripe for picking. Most likely you could sell before the September deadline. Jean had an inspector come and give this place a look-see. I have the report here."

An inspector? Ben glanced around to Mr. Graham, the swirl of the wind beyond the window now in his chest. "Granny was going to sell the inn?"

He couldn't imagine it. Where would he stay when he came home? This was still home. Suddenly, all the old memories floated to the surface, and he felt overwhelmed with affection for this place.

Mr. Graham handed over the inspector's report. It was five pages. New roof, new pool tiles and lining, pool heater, new AC units for the cottages, and in the next year or so, an updated HVAC for the inn. The remaining carpets in Rooms One, Two, and Seven needed to be pulled up, but they covered hardwood, so that was a blessing.

The kitchen appliances were on their last legs, the electrical work would need redoing when the new appliances were installed, and the floor needed to be replaced. The lobby and dining area hardwoods needed to be sanded and polished. The windows were out of code. There were small-ticket items like fixing the door on the storage barn and some loose boards, followed by painting the whole structure. New floors. Thankfully, the plumbing was good to go, as well as the water heaters. Small mercies.

Ben exhaled. This was a lot of work. If he was going to sell, he'd want to get top dollar. His grandparents' memory deserved it. The money would go a long way to helping his parents' mission base. But to get top dollar, he'd have to invest some of his personal funds.

But at the end of it all, could he sell? He felt like he'd be selling his childhood. His teen years. He'd had a lot of laughs in this place. Football team cookouts. The prom after-party. Summer pool parties, if the inn hadn't been too booked.

Helping the thousands of guests who came through the tourist town. Working weddings, and even funerals. He'd saved a toddler who'd fallen into the pool. He'd walked an elderly woman down the path to the pond to spread her beloved husband's ashes.

He'd spearheaded Summer Movie Night, where he'd set up a big screen on the lawn and played classic films like *Battle of Britain* or *North by Northwest*.

Then there was Christmas. The inn was beautiful at Christmas. Romantic. And that was saying something for Ben to use the word. People came from all over to see Granny's decorations.

But the memories were in him, not the bricks and mortar. Nothing could take them from him. To keep the inn, he'd have to live in Hearts Bend and run it. He supposed he could hire someone to manage things, but how could he oversee everything from Sydney?

"What are you thinking, son?" Mr. Graham said.

With the old man's words, the nagging question walked right up and stared Ben in the face. "I don't know." He tucked the inspector's list in the folder. "This was my grandparents' legacy."

"True, but their legacy goes on in your life, in your parents' work. They live on because you live on. Your grandparents' dream doesn't have to be your dream. To be honest, their life's work is just beginning. They got themselves new bodies and are singing praises to the Good Lord with old David and Paul. They might even be making plans to have an inn up in heaven, and I betcha dollars to donuts, they're not even thinking about this place."

Ben laughed. "Betcha you're right." He reached for the photo on the desk. Granddaddy looked so content with the love of his life in his arms, the inn behind him. Granny gazed up at him with so much admiration.

In the private movements of his heart, he knew. *This* was what he wanted more than anything. A love like his grandparents'. More than the adventure of opening hotels around the world, more than the adventure of spearheading the Emerald, he wanted love. True, honest-to-goodness love.

In the last six, seven years, he'd been busy building a life he hoped to give the love of his life. But the job left him without roots, without a chance to find *the one*. Somehow, selling the inn felt like giving up on *the hope* of lasting love.

Yet would he find love in Hearts Bend? Granddaddy had met Granny during a recess game of tag at Hearts Bend Elementary. He'd claimed she'd been one in a million even then. Dad had literally bumped into Mom, spilling coffee all over her, at a mission conference in Johannesburg.

I knew the moment she looked up at me with those wide brown eyes, I loved her.

Too bad love didn't happen like in the movies, where the woman of his dreams would cruise down the inn's driveway looking for a room to rent.

Ben focused on the kind lawyer. "I love this place, Mr. Graham. It's a part of me, and I feel like Granny put its heart and existence in my hands. I can't see a way forward. I can't see a way back."

"Well, in my experience, Ben, and I've had plenty, the answer will make itself known. It might not hurt to talk to Stan at the bank, see what kind of payment scale the bank would take in lieu of foreclosure. Or maybe a refinance. Or..." Mr. Graham slid another folder across the desk. How many of those things did he have? "You could look at this."

An offer to buy the inn. Two hundred thousand. From Frank Hardy.

"Two hundred grand? Is he serious? Just who is this Frank Hardy?"

"Local businessman. He's done a lot for Hearts Bend. He's also Sam Hardy's father."

Ben knew Sam from high school. Sam had been a year ahead, but the superstar had always been good to Ben. Now he was the Titans' quarterback and winning Super Bowls. How had Ben never met his father? In HB, folks knew everyone either from the PTA, the chamber of commerce, the stands of Rock Mill High Friday night football, or sitting next to them in church.

"He wants to buy it for the price of the loan? That's a lowball offer."

"It might be the best you can do with all the repairs. This is prime property, being so close to the new highway connection. Frank will probably tear the place down for something new."

"No." He shot the offer back to Mr. Graham. "I know this place is a mess but, shoot, the land alone is worth more than two hundred grand."

Was that what his grandparents' lifework boiled down to? A debt payoff?

"I can ask around, see if there are any other interested buyers."

"What about Myrtle May, Walt, and Ray?" The front desk receptionist, the cook, and the groundskeeper. They needed something for their loyalty. Not to mention they'd been like family to Ben.

"You hope they managed to save enough for retirement."

If he sold the inn, he'd find a better offer than this Frank Hardy's. He'd want enough for the staff as well as his parents. However, if he didn't sell, he'd have to figure out how to keep this rundown but beloved Hearts Bend landmark running.

That's when Myrtle May burst into the office.

"Ben, you need to— Larry Graham, why, hello." Myrtle May waved, and her brightly colored blue nails wiggled in the air. "I didn't know you were here."

Myrtle May was a walking Christmas tree with her bright red hair, lime green kimono billowing behind her like a superhero cape, purple T-shirt, and white pants. Her toes, painted a wild red, peeped out of her zebra-striped sandals, and her penciled-on eyebrows were always raised in a quizzical expression. Her sweet golden retriever, Bart, entered the room and set his big golden head on Mr. Graham's leg.

"Came to do business with Ben here." Mr. Graham stroked Bart's head. "You're looking mighty fine as always, Myrtle May."

"Larry G., hush up, you're making my heart go pitter-patter." She smiled and tapped his shoulder as she turned to Ben. "Walt's in the kitchen banging pots and muttering about his veggie supplier. I've told him a hundred million times—" She looked at Mr. Graham. "I exaggerate, but you know already."

"Go on."

"I told him to talk to you. There's a supplier in Ashland City who'd be more than happy to sign on with us. I also heard a local guy, JW Namath, was considering selling his produce."

"If you ask me," Mr. Graham said, "Walt just likes to complain. If it's not the vegetable vendor, it's the meat guy or the amount of soap concentration in the stuff he uses for mopping."

Myrtle May made a face at Ben while pointing to Mr. Graham. "Genius, right here, right now."

"Tell me," Mr. Graham said. "Are you two still fighting over who spilled the popcorn at the Bijou in 1964?"

"It was him, I tell you. Hot buttered popcorn all over my brand-new skirt."

"As I recall, that skirt was so short we weren't sure it could be called a skirt."

"Larry Graham, I declare." Myrtle May sputtered a laugh. "I had great legs back then, didn't I?" She wagged her finger under his nose. "Don't answer. Your wife is a good friend of mine. Are you sticking around for lunch?"

"Is it tuna sandwich day?" Mr. Graham stood and stretched his lower back.

"Every Tuesday."

"Then pass." Mr. Graham shook Ben's hand and told him to call him if he needed anything. Then he patted Myrtle's arm. "It's good to see you, old friend."

Ben glanced at his great-aunt. "What's with the tuna sandwich?"

"Don't tell me you can't smell them. They stink to high heaven. Ben, I need you to watch reception for a bit." She pointed in the direction of the desk. "See, I remembered to come tell you. I have a hair appointment this afternoon."

"Thank you," he said. "But I need to know when you take the dog outside too."

"I don't have time. When Bart has to go, he has to go!" With that, she spun on her heel and left singing in her loud, off-key manner. "What a mighty God we serve—" Her voice was, thankfully, cut off by the slamming of the back door.

"She's a force of nature, that one." Mr. Graham chuckled.

"You're telling me." Ben stepped around the desk toward the door. "I'll walk up front with you."

"No need. I'll stop by the kitchen, see if Walt has any

cookies left." He paused at the office door. "I know this news about the inn isn't what you wanted to hear."

"Hardly, Mr. Graham. But I need to decide soon. My boss, a marquee hotel, and my apartment overlooking Sydney Harbor are waiting for me in Sydney."

"Then let Frank Hardy have it for what you owe the bank."

"You can't find an investor, someone to love the place back to life?"

"Seems to me," Mr. Graham said, jutting out his chin, "that's what your granny saw in you."

"Granny told me to live my life, not to worry about this place. She was proud of me."

"Yes, she was. Told me every time we met. 'Guess where Ben is now?' she'd say. 'Budapest. Can you believe it?'"

"Mr. Graham, I'm asking, what would she want me to do?"

"Well, son, I can only guess based on our forty years of friendship and singing with her in the church choir, but I think she'd want you to talk to the Lord about it. He—"

"The Lord and I aren't exactly on speaking terms."

"I see." His lips turned down in disapproval. "Then take this summer to grow up and reconcile. Does a body no good to cut off the One who knows you better than you know yourself. He's got a plan."

Really? Because when Ben's parents left him in Hearts Bend twenty-six years ago, he'd been pretty sure God didn't care a thing about him.

CHAPTER 3

*C*ami startled awake at the blaring horn of a tornado warning. Stumbling to the living room, clicking on lights, she found the remote and turned on the weather news.

The meteorologist said a funnel cloud had been spotted about two miles from downtown. Cami perched on the edge of her sofa and watched the images outside her building move closer. She had an emergency bag prepped and stored in the front closet. If she had to evacuate, she'd grab the bag and run downstairs to the basement.

By the time the storm had blown over, she was wired with adrenaline. The day's first lights broke over the city, and she decided to just get the day going. She showered and dressed, made a green smoothie, then collected her things and headed out.

Call her crazy, but she'd let Keith Niven talk her into visiting the Hearts Bend Inn. She'd been awash with sentiment as he talked about Vern and Jean Carter's legacy and how much the town loved and needed the inn.

Images of her summer weekends painting with Mama filled

her. If she closed her eyes, she was twelve, fourteen, fifteen again. They'd eaten breakfast in their cottage, Cottage Three, then walked to Ella's Diner for an early dinner.

Mama had always ordered a salad. Cami had always ordered a burger, fries, and vanilla shake. She'd swum in the pool, walked the grounds, and oh, how could she forget? Kissed that boy Ben in the tree house.

Her phone jingled with her assistant's ringtone. "Astrid, I'll be in late. Running down to Hearts Bend to check out the inn."

"I'm not going to ask why, but I need some questions answered when you get back."

"I'll be there before lunch."

On a whim, Cami put together a proposal of nine hundred thousand dollars, which felt extremely generous. She suspected the place needed massive renovations. Which was not the typical Akron acquisition.

They bought properties to tear down and build new. Or to sell to new investors when the market increased. In all her years with the company, Cami couldn't remember any renovation projects. But no one could deny there was a market for that kind of work.

She told herself the inn was a different project altogether. It was her project. Mama's inn. For the first time in well over a decade, she wanted to remember her beautiful, kind, sweet, artistic mother. It had to be thoughts of the inn.

Forty minutes and one Starbucks grande latte later, Cami turned her BMW down Hearts Bend Inn's long, tree-lined driveway and chose a parking spot. Shutting off the engine, she peered through the windshield toward the old building, which stirred even more buried memories.

Cami popped open her door and stepped out, grabbing her attaché case. The inn sat in the glimmering afternoon sunlight, and she felt as if she'd awakened from a long-forgotten dream.

For a moment, just a moment, Mama stood next to her with her paints in hand. *Isn't it beautiful here, Cami?*

In the distance a chain saw hummed, and a hint of sawdust scented the clean air. Cami moved toward the large, wrap-around porch, caught between the girl she'd been and the woman she'd become.

On first glance, she saw the porch needed a bit of work. The rocking chairs, although inviting, were a bit worn, but a beautiful floral wreath hung on the door.

The inn's wood siding was new but needed a fresh coat of paint. The flower beds were filled with colorful blooms but needed to be weeded. Mama would have been on her hands and knees pulling those weeds, never mind the dirt that would build up under her nails.

Mrs. Carter, the inn's owner, had always been proud of her gardens. Mama had loved to set up her easel and paint—

Stop. She had not come here to walk entirely down memory lane. She mentally took off her daughter hat and put on her business hat. She'd worked hard to forget the past, even the good.

Then what was she doing here? Why would she even consider buying this place? She blamed the smooth-talking Keith Niven.

"Can I help you?" An older man in denim overalls and a white T-shirt lumbered forward. His white hair curled wildly around a fisherman's hat, which shaded his face. Was that Ray, the gardener who'd been here back in the day? He had to be in his seventies by now.

"Just checking out the inn."

"Well, go on in. Myrtle May will set you right."

She reached for the door handle as the chain saw fell silent, then quickly hummed and buzzed again.

Cami wasn't ready for the impact of the familiar, homey

lobby. She drew in a deep breath, hand to her middle, as the memories threatened to break loose. She suddenly closed her eyes, not wanting to see, not wanting to remember.

Oh, this might have been a really bad idea. But then a wafting, sweet aroma of cinnamon and sugar almost toppled her. The cookies. How she'd craved the cookies over the years. They still made them?

"Well, land sakes, who do we have here?" A tall, slender woman with bottle-red hair, bright clothes, and her smiling face covered in makeup crossed the lobby to the registration desk. Her huge smile was welcoming and oddly familiar. "Cami Jackson, is that you? My, my, you sure grew up pretty. But I knew you would, yes siree, I knew you would. Just like your mama."

"Myrtle May." Wrapped in her business persona, she stepped toward the woman, hand outstretched.

"One and the same." A whiff of Chanel No. 5 nearly overwhelmed Cami. "Welcome home, girl." The woman grabbed her in a powerful embrace. "About time."

Cami stiffened against her cheerful warmth, but then the way she made her feel—like family—encouraged her to relax and hug Myrtle May back.

After Mama died, all the warmth, heart, and traditions evaporated from the Jackson household. Her maternal grandparents had died when Cami was young, and Dad's parents tried to keep in touch, but they'd retired in England after Grandpa Jay finished his assignment for the Army. Dad stopped taking them to church, and life became a stoic routine of school, homework, dinner, and bedtime. No stories, no singing, no playing in the summer rain. No Hearts Bend Inn.

Myrtle May stepped back and held Cami at arm's length, giving her a deep inspection. "I know it's been fifteen years, but my, my, my, you're a sight for sore eyes. Your mama was a blessing to Vern and Jean and me. We always looked forward to your painting weekends." Myrtle May gently swept Cami's bangs aside, her soft fingertips grazing Cami's forehead. Cami gritted her jaw against a surge of tears and steeled her heart. One more touch, one more word, and she'd lose it. Right here. Right now. This was a mistake. A big mistake. "You have her beautiful eyes. Like dark chocolate."

"So I'm told." Cami's low reply was thick and heavy as she freed herself from the woman's grip.

"But you're dressed like your father. Even carrying one of those fancy briefcases." Myrtle May laughed and wagged her finger at Cami. "Chip off the old block. Good for you."

Was it, though? For the first time, Cami felt challenged in her soul. But that was Myrtle May—all Southern charm and sharp words.

"What brings you to town, Cami?" Myrtle May moved behind the registration desk. The same one she'd leaned against as Mama checked them into Cottage Three, then chatted with Mrs. Carter about anything and everything. "Can I book you in a room? Cottage Three is out of commission right now, but we have a lovely, relatively remodeled room on the third floor. Great view of the garden."

"No, um, thank you." Cami smiled, fighting all sorts of foreign emotions. "I'm looking for the owner."

"Well, of course. Should've known you'd want to see Ben." Myrtle May walked her to the door. "He's the one making all that ruckus with the chain saw. Should've heard him belly-aching about taking down that old oak tree. You'd think he cut off his own arm."

"The one with the tree house?" Cami looked toward the side of the porch where the tree had stood. "We were sitting up there when the boards cracked and the whole thing fell apart. We tumbled to the ground."

Teach her to kiss a boy in a rickety tree house.

"One and the same. Last night's storm toppled it. I told Ben to be grateful it didn't land on the inn."

So, Ben Carter was the owner? She'd not thought of him in years. Any thoughts of him had been locked away with all her other memories of Hearts Bend and the inn.

He had been the "love of her life" from the moment she'd seen him. But what had she known when she was six? The summer they were fifteen, though... She'd given her first kiss to the tall, gangly teen.

On second thought, his kiss had been awesome. She smiled, watching the memory of how they'd fallen and hit the ground with a thud.

"He's right over there." Myrtle May gave her a gentle push forward.

The ground between the inn and the tree was spongy from last night's storm. She'd been smart enough to wear sensible shoes today, or what she thought were sensible shoes—her Valentino calfskin wedges.

Ben's back was to her as he worked the chain saw through leafy branches. Cami assembled the business persona Myrtle May had dismantled, ready to talk business with her old friend Ben.

Sawdust peppered the air as he worked the saw through a large limb. When it hit the ground, he stood back, cut off the saw, and pushed his goggles to the top of his blue Tennessee Titans ball cap.

"Ben?" she said. "Ben Carter?"

He turned, the chain saw swinging from his hand. "Yes?"

Cami halted mid-step. The man facing her was *not* the boy she remembered.

He wore a T-shirt, work jeans, boots, a Titans hat with the bill in the back. His bright blue eyes mesmerized her, his high cheeks were pink from a day in the hot sun, and a reddish-blond stubble covered his jaw. His chest and arms were broad and muscled, covered in sawdust, and she was...staring way too long.

"Ben Carter." She approached, hand outstretched, ready for a firm, businesswoman handshake. "Hi, I'm Cami—"

"Jackson." He stared at her through a narrowed gaze and gestured toward his gloved, dusty hands holding the saw. "It's been a long time."

"Yes, yes it has." She lowered her hand, brushing it against her skirt. "H-how have you been?"

"Good. You?"

"Also good, though I'm sorry about your granny. She was always so kind and sweet to Mama and me."

"She couldn't do or be anything else."

"So, you're the owner now?"

"I am." Ben settled the chain saw against the tree and removed his goggles. "Did you come for your mom's painting?"

"I came to— What? Mom's painting?"

"The one in the lobby. It's actually been on loan to us. I think it was a gift for your dad. Birthday, anniversary, but after —" Ben's voice trailed off.

"She died..." She could say it. The two little words that had changed her life.

"Yeah. He told Granny to keep it, hang it in the lobby." He removed his gloves and slapped them against his jeans.

"The painting in the lobby was a gift for my dad?" She hadn't even noticed the painting. How could she not recognize Mama's work? Had she forgotten already? The idea made her sick.

Mama's last summer, they'd booked into Cottage Three every weekend. Annalise had been working for college spending money, and Dad had turned into the Brant Jackson Cami knew today, so it had just been the two of them. While

Mama had worked on a large canvas, Cami had painted several smaller, much less impressive pictures.

Mom would pause, lean over from her position facing the southwest corner of the inn's grounds, and inspect Cami's work, her brush poised elegantly in her hand. Her favorite spot had been the small opening in the garden where they could see the barn. Mama had painted her final few pictures in that spot.

Darling, you're getting so good. I love the colors and the way your brushstrokes create movement.

Movement. That's how she felt every time she painted. Moved. Like she was telling the stories of her heart even she didn't know existed.

"Am I right?" Ben stepped closer, lifting his sweaty T-shirt from his lean abdomen. "She wanted to hide the painting in plain sight. When your dad walked in, she wondered if he'd notice it."

The memory came rushing back. The large canvas pastoral scene of a field with waving grass, wild sunflowers, trees, blue skies, and the edge of the red barn. The bench. Mama had loved that bench.

"He was coming down for his birthday."

"She died that weekend." The words sounded sad, but time had distanced her from the emotion. Dad had been three hours late that night. Caught up in a golf game and dinner with a potential client. He'd forgotten his own birthday dinner.

"Granny said one of you would come for it one day." He peered at her with such a sincere blue. "Is that why you're here?"

"No, it's not." Cami wanted to sit, process, give her shaking legs a break. Some of her buried memories knocked, their mocking voices crying within. There was no place to land except the ground, so she remained standing, planted. "I had no idea that painting was for my father. In fact, I'd forgotten all about it." Like everything else associated with Hearts Bend Inn.

"Then why are you here?"

"I, um..." *Gather yourself.* "I came to talk business."

Ben glanced toward the inn, then back at Cami. "Business? What sort of business?"

"Buying the inn. I've come with a proposal."

"You want to buy the inn?" His grin made her wobble all the more. "Is that why you're dressed for a board meeting?"

"I work for Akron Development. I've managed to become one of the company's top closers."

Was that admiration in his eyes?

"I'm not surprised. Do you still paint?"

"No time." She was finding herself, the Akron woman, not the artist girl. She was Dad's girl now, not Mama's.

"Who told you I was selling?"

"Word gets out."

"Cami, to be honest, I don't know what I'm doing. Still trying to figure it out. But let me rinse off and I'll at least give you a tour."

She followed him to the back of the property, toward the barn and work shed, rehearsing her pitch, the one she'd practiced yesterday and again on the drive over.

The Ben she'd known had never wanted to own the inn. He'd had plans and dreams to travel the world. Didn't want anything to tie him down.

At a short water spigot, Ben yanked off his T-shirt and knelt to rinse off. Cami tried not to stare, really. But seriously, those abs had not come from sitting on the couch binge-watching Netflix.

After a few minutes, he rose up and ran his hand through his reddish-blond hair, then reached inside the shed for a towel.

He dried off, returned the towel to the shed, and came out with a clean, dry T-shirt and his ball cap back on.

"You have a change of clothes in the shed?"

"Myrtle May set me up out here. She said I can't come in her lobby all sweaty and dirty."

"She runs a tight ship."

"She's all right, MM. She was the only one there for Granny in the end..." His voice trailed off, and Cami felt his regret. "Anyway, I'll show you around." He walked backward toward the pool, regarding her. "You really want to buy the place? It needs a lot of work."

"The need for renovations is reflected in my offer."

Did Ben want to sell? She couldn't tell. But he was so much like the Ben she'd crushed on every summer. Older, of course, broader, more handsome, but with the same calm interior she'd loved.

"The pool needs new tile and liner but otherwise is in good shape." Ben paused by the kiddie end. The blue water sparkled in the sunlight, highlighting the tile that needed replacing as well as the teak lounge chairs and umbrellas, which were sun-bleached and old.

Next they took a paved path to a huge flower garden. Yellow daffodils lifted their cheery heads toward the summer sun. At the end of the garden, there were three walkways to three small cottages. Cottages One and Two were single bedrooms and baths. Cottage Three was the largest with two bedrooms, each with a clawfoot tub and an old farmers sink fifteen years ago, popular well before HGTV made it a thing. But she'd avoid that space for now. She was doing well, holding on, but she had no guarantee if she walked near or into Cottage Three.

The owner's house was beyond the cottages, centered in the middle of a tree grove. The three-bedroom farmhouse was modest, but with all the outdoor space, it could be a charming place to raise a family.

The cottages and the farmhouse backed up to a pond with a dock and a garden-sized windmill.

Cami had spent numerous summer evenings sitting on the edge of the dock with Ben, toes skimming the water, talking, dreaming, his arm barely grazing hers, sometimes swimming, often rowing out to the middle in a small boat. It'd taken him all summer to kiss her in that tree house. The memories made her laugh.

"Care to share?" Ben said, turning to her.

"I was remembering the tree house."

He grinned and pushed the hat back on his head. "I kept thinking, 'What a kiss! We broke the tree house.'"

Their laughter harmonized with reminiscing.

"Then lost our breath when we hit the ground," Cami said.

"I'll tell you one thing, I've never been kissed like that since."

"Well then, we have that in common." Cami stepped toward the pond. "I forgot how beautiful it is here." She glanced back at him. "My offer is fair."

"Maybe, but who says I'm going to sell?"

She faced him, arms akimbo. "Me."

He glanced around as if looking for someone. "Really? Because I don't see your army."

"Well, Ben Carter, that's because I'm an army unto myself." She loved that she made him laugh.

Ben stepped toward her, and without asking her permission, her heart skipped a few beats. "Is that so?" he said. "Because—"

Cami's phone chimed from her bag. "Excuse me, let me make sure it's not my assistant."

She knew full well it wasn't Astrid—she had a specific

ring—but she needed a moment to figure out what was going on with her. Heart flutters as she walked down memory lane at Hearts Bend Inn. Remembering Mama without falling apart.

She'd come here to do business, but once she'd stepped onto the grounds, the daughter inside of her had yearned to be heard.

The text was from Meghan, Cami's favorite associate at the shoe boutique she loved to frequent. *Shoe sale this weekend. Ten percent off Louboutin, Prada, Choo, and Blahnik.* At the moment, shoes were the farthest thing from her mind. Which meant miracles did happen.

She took a moment to respond. This would be her last sale with this shop. From now on she'd have to find shoes in Indy.

Tucking her phone away, she turned to see Ben next to her. "I just realized Cottage Three was the one you shared with your mom." He raised his hat off his head and settled it back down. Apparently, he wasn't comfortable with this either. "I take it you've not been back since."

"I've not, no." Cami walked on. "Can we tour the inn?"

As they approached, she could see the shutters were slightly crooked and paint-chipped.

Ben led her to the back door and gestured for Cami to go first. "The kitchen," he said. "Needs work but I won't give you the nitty-gritty."

The hall led them past the kitchen, where they were greeted by a huge golden retriever. A wide smile spread across the aging dog's face.

"This is Bart, Myrtle May's most recent rescue. She adopts aging dogs and gives them their forever home."

"Makes you love her all the more, doesn't it?"

Myrtle May danced down the hallway. "Howdy again, Cami. Ben, I need to take Bart for a walk." She followed Bart out the front door, her raspy voice singing, *"Blessed assurance, Jesus is mine.* Oh, what a foretaste of glory divine!"

"You can see why she was never offered a recording contract," Ben said. "But she gives the place atmosphere."

Was he doing it on purpose? Charming her. And where had he been the last fifteen years? She didn't see a ring or a ring tan line, so she assumed he wasn't married. But in love? Engaged? Entangled?

Cami paused by a large bulletin board posted outside the kitchen. Papers of every color and size were haphazardly pinned to it. Apartment for rent, dinner specials at Angelo's, Fourth of July at the Scott Farm, and a huge flyer announcing the square dance next weekend at the old community barn.

"The lobby furniture is relatively new," Ben said, and Cami followed him into the open space of the lobby. "But the rest needs a bit of work."

Cami walked behind the sofa, which faced the large wood-burning fireplace. "I sat here in the lobby with Mama and Dad and my sister one Christmas Eve. Didn't your grandparents go all out?"

"Every year, without fail."

"We had so much fun," Cami said. "We didn't know it'd be our last—" The memory lane tour must end. None of it would bring Mom back or restore the years since. Memory lane wouldn't change what had transpired with Dad. She was here to do business. "What kind of business does the inn do?"

"To be honest, not a lot. The books are a mess, but I'll get into it. Granny was the charm of the inn. Granddaddy was the businessman. After he died, things got lax."

"I understand." Her entire family had let things go, every-thing really, after Mom died. Took Cami years to figure out who she was, who she wanted to be.

Cami inspected the bookshelves where guests left behind

their paperbacks. On the oak table was a book on Tennessee wildflowers.

"I think you'll find my offer is fair." She turned toward the reception desk, and that's when she saw it. Mama's painting. The pastoral scene of the inn's grounds showing a silhouetted couple in the bottom third. They sat on a wrought iron bench, his arm lovingly around her shoulders, their heads leaned together.

"That's the painting," Ben said.

"Yeah, I know. I watched her paint it." The emotions swirling in her were sentimental, messy, and chaotic. "The bench..." She stepped toward the painting. "The bench in the garden... It's gone."

"Don't know what happened to it. I can't remember when I last saw it." Ben stood next to her. His warm skin carried the scent of sawdust. "When I was in college, maybe."

"College? Where'd you go?"

"UT."

"What? I was a Georgia Dawg."

"Well, I won't hold *that* against you. I bet you were one of the cool people. I was in my dorm studying, wishing I was cool."

"You were always the coolest, Ben." Cami shook her head and stared back at the painting.

Mama was gone. The bench was gone. In a few months, she'd be gone. But this inn? It had to remain.

"Ben?" She fixed on a smile, swallowed her feelings, and turned to Ben. "Let me show you my offer."

Ben was starting to loathe folders. He settled onto the couch in the lobby of the inn and stared at the folder. This one from

Cami was worth a look. She'd morphed from the girl he used to know into a hardened businesswoman.

"The offer is more than fair. I can email you a copy if you give me your card." Cami's professional smile splashed across her face like a million-watt light.

As she held out the blue folder, he hesitated. Did he want to know? Was he ready to sell? Despite the pressure to return to Sydney, he wanted to do right by his grandparents' legacy. His legacy.

Then there was this woman, Cami Jackson, pricking his curiosity. She'd been his first major crush. His first kiss. He had a memory of her loose hair glinting in the sun as she sat on the lawn painting with her mother.

Now her dark curls were slicked back into a sleek ponytail, her business suit looked tailor-made, and she carried the same case as the European director of VJR had in Italy last year. And she never did anything cheap.

Life and death had changed her. Just like it was changing him.

She was beautiful, with her eyes the color of coffee—the good stuff, not Walt's mud—and a charming smile she worked with expertise. Bet she won a lot of deals for Akron.

If he opened this folder, would she turn all of her charm on him? He might not survive.

"Ben?" She waved the folder, then set it on the table in front of him. "Nine hundred thousand. All cash. We close in a week."

He snapped up the folder. Take that, Frank Hardy. "Cash?"

"Is that a yes?" Yep, there was *that* smile.

"No, not yet." He closed his eyes and braced for her best pitch. But he needed to think. Close in a week? Why the rush? "What do you want to do with this place?"

"Fair question. Akron is not in the restoration business, but I've been wanting to acquire some different projects. The inn could be my test project."

She hesitated like she wanted to say something, and for a moment her professional persona waned and he could see the girl he remembered.

"What are you not saying? Do you doubt your idea?" If he was going to sell, he had to make sure he sold to the right person. Even if that person was Cami Jackson. He set the folder on the table, not ready to hold on to it.

"Nothing. I was going to say no—" She laughed softly. "I'd never vocalized my idea to acquire small projects for Akron. Felt good to say it. Ben, I know this place means a lot to you. Me too. But more than our sentiment, the inn is a good property and has a lot of potential."

He considered her confession. Then, "But Akron has a reputation of tearing things down. You know, pave paradise, put up a parking lot." He'd gotten an earful from Granny when Akron bid on the Wedding Shop downtown. They'd wanted that corner for a parking lot. She'd been hopping mad.

That Brant Jackson is going to knock it to the ground. Why, I bought my wedding dress from Cora in '56.

"You can't just tear down history," he added.

"You're right, Akron does tend to tear old buildings down to make room for new development projects. But not always. This will be my acquisition, and I don't intend to tear it down." Her hesitation was gone, and her professionalism was locked back into place. "If you keep the inn, what are you going to do with it? What do you do for a living, by the way?"

"I work for Viridian Jewel Resorts. I open hotels for them around the world. I'm supposed to be in Sydney right now setting up to open our South Pacific marquee hotel. The Emerald. Got a great view of the Opera House. If all goes well, I'll be opening a second resort in Hong Kong next year."

"Viridian." She arched her brow. "Very nice."

Ah, so he'd impressed her. The VJR had a reputation of five-star quality. Jobs with them were as coveted as a night in one of the resorts.

"How long have you been with them? Dad tried to acquire one of their older hotels, but they refused to negotiate."

"Their properties never depreciate, if you can believe it. I've been with them seven years. Started not long after college. I've opened marquee hotels in Budapest, London, Manhattan."

"But you should be in Sydney?"

"My director gave me the summer to take care of Granny's estate. But I'm answering emails and texts all night long."

She grinned. "I bet. You can't open a marquee hotel for Viridian when you're halfway around the world." She picked up her folder and offered it to him again. "It's a good offer, Ben. Accept it and you're on a plane back to Australia by the end of the week. You don't have any other worthy offers."

"I should ask how you know that, but you'll tell me you did your homework."

"Keith Niven told me." Her smile was genuine, not the practiced one that could seal a deal. He liked her real one even better. "He said he'd tried to get some people interested in case you wanted to sell. No one would bite, so he called me. He knew I used to come here as a kid."

"I had an offer from Frank Hardy, but it was very lowball." Ben reached for the folder again. "My grandparents devoted their lives to the inn. Got married in '56, bought this place in '59, the year Dad was born. Selling makes me feel like—" A rotten grandson. It was bad enough he'd not been there for Granny when she needed him. Now to sell her beloved inn?

"Makes you feel like a bad grandson?" So, the girl with

gorgeous eyes was also a mind reader. "Life goes on. You can't stay in the past. This was your grandparents' life work. Yours is with Viridian. Go, enjoy, have fun. Live *your* life and sell me this place."

"True, but are you going to take care of it personally? Keep an eye on things? What are you going to do with the inn?"

"I won't be in charge of the property personally. I'm heading to Indianapolis, but it'll be good, trust me."

He laughed. "Solid answer, Jackson." He handed back the blue folder. "Thanks, but no thanks."

"What? I'd think you'd recognize a good deal when you see one. You can't just let the inn sit here and go to rot." She shoved the folder at him again. "Do you have the money to pay the bank loan?"

"So you know about the loan too?"

"Give me a few more days and I'll tell you your shoe size."

He laughed. "The great Cami Jackson knows all."

"Tell you what. Take some time to think it over. You have forty-eight hours." Cami extended her hand to Ben.

Her grip was firm and confident, and fit perfectly with his. He had a crazy urge to hold on to her a bit longer. But she pulled free and turned for the door.

"Call me."

"I've got your number." He held up the folder.

Watching her go, Ben wished he was fifteen again, sitting with her in the tree house, leaning in for a kiss.

With a sigh, he dropped to the desk chair and reviewed her offer. It was a good offer. He bet he could negotiate some, get a higher price. He'd divide the money between his parents and Myrtle May. She could buy a small house in town. He'd set aside some for Walt and Ray.

"Well, well, all your barking at me about leaving the reg desk vacant, I return to find you in here and not out front."

Ben jumped up. "Oh man, I totally forgot. I was talking to Cami and—"

"She's a nice girl," Myrtle May said. "Beautiful, don't you think?"

The woman was fishing, but he wasn't biting. He held up the folder. "She wants to buy the inn."

Myrtle May stepped back, eyes wide. "Really? What did you say?"

"That I wasn't sure. But she wants an answer in forty-eight hours."

"Well, goodness, she doesn't give a man much time."

True, but life never gave a man much time.

CHAPTER 4

*B*en's computer chimed again with another incoming email. Seventy-three emails and counting. Not to mention two calls from his boss in the last hour. Jim had made it very clear Ben needed to be in Sydney as soon as possible. Ben guessed he regretted giving him the summer to finalize his grandmother's—no, *his*—estate.

Jordan's multiple emails cemented Ben was needed Down Under.

Ben, is there any way you can get here earlier? I know you have your grandmother's estate, but things are moving fast. Jordan.

Ben, here are the applications for the reception staff. I need your top forty by the end of the week. I'll set up Zoom interviews. Jordan.

No rest for the weary. Ben downloaded the zip file, then stared at the cookie he'd stolen from the pantry. He'd missed dinner, but the cookie held no appeal.

After Cami had left, he'd gone back to work, cutting up his "memory" tree. He'd stacked the branches to use for firewood, but the trunk could be milled for lumber. Cole Danner was picking it up tomorrow. In exchange, Cole would give him lumber back for repairs around the inn.

Speaking of repairs... He spied the inspector's folder under Cami's blue one. Note to self: Ban the use of folders at the Emerald.

The weight of the last few weeks settled on him. If this were just any ole inn, a place he didn't love and treasure, he'd sell in a heartbeat. No question. Cami's offer was fair. There was a huge part of him that wanted to do just that. Let it go. Get on with his life. If all went well with the Emerald and Hong Kong, he might make South Pacific regional director. One director bonus check was more than he'd make in ten years running Hearts Bend Inn.

As it stood now, he made a good salary. Viridian paid for his apartment and gave him a food stipend to eat from resort kitchens. He was able to tuck a little into savings and send financial support to his parents. But if he made director—

Was that the answer? Work hard, get to regional director, and fund the inn's repairs? But that'd be at least another three to five years. He'd have to hire a staff to run the inn. Could he find trustworthy folks? How could he keep an eye on things when he was so far away?

Then there was the matter of the debt. His savings account was generous but not quite up to two hundred grand.

There were his folks. Now in their early sixties, they might be ready to come off the mission field. They could live at the inn. Run things. Though Dad had never once expressed any interest in the family business. In fact, he'd run from this place the moment he graduated from high school. Said he had a different calling on his life.

"What should I do, Dad?"

The tenor of his father's voice resonated across his heart.

Sell, follow your calling.

Then again, Dad didn't fully grasp how the inn had saved Ben.

Enough. Brooding never helped, so Ben stirred himself, reached for the cookie, and started working through the rest of his emails.

Besides the applications, Jordan had sent twelve more emails, four with problems and the solutions already outlined. All he needed was Ben's approval.

Jim's emails always required research, and emails from the builder, engineer, city inspectors, health inspectors, and insurance agency were packed full of questions and information.

Another email from Jordan dropped into his inbox. He was in the office bright and early.

After the Hong Kong call, Jim is going to be on-site to check on our progress.

For the first time since he'd arrived in Hearts Bend, Ben felt the stress. He really needed to be in Sydney. The entire resort chain was holding their breath on this one. The opening *must* be a success.

Ben peeked at Cami's folder. He was asking for a solution, and here it was staring him in the face. So why turn it down?

Take the offer and get back to your real job.

Cami had given him forty-eight hours, and ten hours had already ticked off the clock.

From the lobby, the front door chime sounded. The doors locked at 10:00 p.m., so new guests had to ring the bell.

Ben found an older couple waiting on the porch, arm in arm, the man wheeling a small suitcase behind him. They were dressed in their Sunday best—the woman even wore a small red hat pinned into her gray hair.

"We've a reservation. Room Twelve." The man stretched out his hand in a greeting.

Ben shook his hand, escorted them to the reservation desk. "Let's see...Mr. and Mrs. Walker? We have you for two nights with the honeymoon package." Myrtle May and the house-keeper went all out for the honeymoon guests—which they didn't get very often if Granny's records were accurate. "Complete with bubbly and chocolate-dipped strawberries."

"We're not really honeymooners." The woman looked up at her husband. "But it's our anniversary. We honeymooned here forty-eight years ago. We were young and didn't have a lot of extra cash, so we took a little day trip from Knoxville to Hearts Bend for a town festival. We had a flat tire just outside of town. Dan got soaked trying to put on the spare. Turned out it was flat too."

"We thought we'd have to spend the entire night in the car," the man said. "It was raining so hard we had no choice but to leave the windows rolled up and—"

"It was like a sauna, even with all the rain." The woman looked as in love as ever. "Finally, a police officer drove by. He arranged for a tow truck, and they brought us here while the car was in the shop."

"We looked like drowned rats!" The man's laugh was youthful and energetic. "The owners put us up, free of charge. Said they kept a room just for situations like ours."

The woman motioned to the upright piano shoved against the wall on the other side of the fireplace. "His wife played for us while the husband rustled us up some dinner and sweet tea."

"Best dinner I ever had," the man said. "Do you remember their names, honey? I thought I'd never forget, but I didn't factor in old age."

"Jean and Vern Carter," Ben said.

"That's right," the woman said. "You knew them?"

"They were my grandparents."

"Lucky you." The man patted the desk surface with his hand. "How are they doing?"

"Granddaddy died six years ago and Granny...last month."

"Oh, I'm so sorry," the woman said sincerely. "You'll see them again, take comfort."

Okay, but wasn't that thought a bit of a cliché?

"This life is passing. But the next life—"

"Let me get you signed in." Ben asked for their credit card and handed them a registration packet. He'd heard the messages of life, death, heaven, and hell. Seen more miracles than most. He'd read the Bible verses, argued about them with Dad, and in the moment, didn't want to relive it all over again. Church, religion, wasn't for everyone.

The man, Mr. Walker, signed the credit card transaction, then reached down for his luggage. "Are you running the place now?"

"For the time being."

"We've remembered this place our whole lives," Mrs. Walker said. "Your grandparents' kindness was life changing. Our stay here is Walker family lore. One we've told over and over to our kids and grandkids. Oh, Dan, I'm sorry now we didn't make it back to tell the Carters." She peered at Ben. "We'd always planned to come back, but then the kids started coming, and we were working, raising a family. Next thing you know, it's forty-eight years later."

"But this anniversary our kids sent us back." Mr. Walker was busting his buttons. "We raised some great kids, Barb."

The Walkers shot heart eyes at each other. Their happiness and love were palpable, like Ben could reach out and touch it. Their memory of Granddaddy and Granny washed over him with sentimentality.

Never once as the hotel manager at any of the Viridian

Jewel Resorts had Ben offered rooms to those in need or inter-acted with such a sweet couple.

He rarely, if ever, met the same guests twice. Business trav-elers, sometimes, if the timing was right. But honeymooning couples? Families taking an extravagant excursion? No, never. And forget about offering shelter to someone in trouble.

The rooms had to earn a specific amount. The food, earn a certain profit.

The profit margin was a part of the hotel business he didn't like. The guests were just numbers. A way to meet the resort's bottom line.

"Here is your room key as well as a key to the front door. We lock up every night at ten. Open every morning at six." Ben handed Mr. Walker an old-fashioned metal key. Were he to stay here and run the inn, he'd upgrade to keycards. But he wasn't taking over, was he? "And at Hearts Bend Inn, we insist on helping you to your room."

Ben walked around the desk to help the Walkers with their luggage. Service was the Viridian culture. Escorting guests to their rooms was the Golden Rule.

Checking to make sure everything was shipshape, he bid the Walkers goodnight and returned to the lobby. It was late and he really needed to get to bed, but a mountain of VJR work waited for him back in the office.

Coffee. He needed coffee. Even a cup of Walt's horrible brew would do. Which reminded him—check with Java Jane's about supplying the inn with coffee.

At the registration desk, he checked to make sure he'd cleared the Walkers' form, then turned off the lobby lights except for the wall sconces.

The warm, low glow of the lights triggered a store of memo-ries. How many times had he checked in a solo traveler caught in a storm or a weary family who'd come to town for the Fourth of July festival or summer tourism?

Then there'd been the January of 2010, when he'd come home for Granddaddy's birthday and Old Man Winter had dumped almost ten inches of snow on them. Ben had checked in quite a few stranded travelers. His grandparents had opened all the rooms and cottages and fired up the kitchen to feed anyone who needed something to eat. Granddaddy had grilled up all the meat he could, and Granny had made batch after batch of cookies. Ben himself had stirred up several gallons of hot chocolate, tea, and coffee.

The fireplace had roared with hot flames, and one of the guests had sat at the piano, playing request after request.

We're having us a slumber party, Granny had said.

Ben laughed softly, remembering her expression, hearing the excitement in her voice.

Then there was the family who'd lost their house in a fire. Granny had given them Cottage One for six months. Free.

The young woman on the run from an abuser.

Aunt Myrtle May when she found herself a widow at fifty-five with no place to go.

During high school, the inn had burst at the seams during the spring and summer, especially the Fourth of July weekend, and again for Christmas holidays.

He'd worked twelve-hour days all summer, but he'd loved it. Granddaddy had taken every opportunity to teach him about the inn and the business.

The inn wasn't just a place to lay one's head; it was a shelter, a respite, a home away from home. His grandparents had made sure people were comfortable and safe. They'd made sure *Ben* was comfortable and safe.

The interaction with the Walkers reminded him of why

he'd started in the hotel business—the gratification of helping people. Of being the port in a storm.

When he'd interviewed with Viridian, they'd offered him excitement and travel. So far, they'd delivered in spades. But he hadn't realized how much he missed the sweet interactions with guests.

"Ben?" Mr. Walker walked toward him holding an antique doorknob. "This came off the bathroom door."

"I am so sorry." He'd have to check all the doorknobs. Myrtle May said Ray had a lifetime of supplies out in the barn. "Do you want to change rooms?"

"No." Mr. Walker winked. "After all, we are on our forty-eighth honeymoon."

Ben tried not to laugh. "Yes, sir." What else could he say? *Enjoy? Have a nice night? Go get 'em, tiger?* But in a small way, he envied the man. He had true love. Ben couldn't remember the last time he'd been on a date.

The inn, unlike the Emerald, or any of the hotels he'd opened, had a history. The inn was *his* history. No one would remember who opened the Emerald or any of the properties in London or Budapest.

But the Walkers remembered his grandparents almost fifty years later. Granddaddy used to say, *You can't take it with you, but you can leave it behind.*

What was Ben leaving behind? What did he want his legacy to be? What was his calling? Helping the rich and famous book a spa or limo? Climbing the corporate ladder? Nothing wrong with any of it *if* it was his calling.

The UT fight song sounded from the office where he'd left his phone. Ben hurried to answer. Jordan. On FaceTime. This could only mean trouble.

"You know you owe me." Cami tapped the brakes. Nashville's crazy I-65 rush-hour traffic slowed to a crawl again as she and Annalise made their way toward Cumberland Oasis, Nashville's poshest country club on the river. It had been five days since Cami had heard from Ben. He had completely ignored her offer. She squeezed the steering wheel and tapped at her brakes again. Ugh, traffic. Thankfully, the exit was coming up in a few miles.

"I know, and I'm grateful." Annalise brushed on mascara in the light of the visor mirror, then stuffed the tube in her small makeup tote. "I just need a second set of eyes and ears on this one."

"Is she a bridezilla?"

"Not really, but she has a lot of ideas." Annalise sat back with a sigh. "She texts me every day with something new and different. She's very invested."

Was it Cami's imagination or did Annalise have bags under her eyes? Her sister's normally pristine hair was pulled back with barrettes, and since when did she put makeup on in the car? It wasn't like she hadn't had time to get ready at home.

"What's going on with you? I haven't talked to you since you closed the Emerson deal." Annalise pulled out some lipstick and gazed into the mirror again.

"Busy, figuring out the move to Indy, interviewing people, talking to Realtors, the contractor. And why are you putting on makeup in my car?"

"The day got away from me." Annalise snapped the lipstick back in the tube. "I still can't wrap my head around the idea of you moving. Dad never said a word to me."

"Nor me before I was in his office."

"What am I going to do without you?" Annalise said. "I asked Steve if we could move to Indy. He's working from home most of the time, so why not? But my career is most definitely here. I don't want to start a wedding planning business in a new city."

Annalise was well on her way to becoming one of Nashville's top wedding planners. She'd worked hard to build her reputation. Thus, the appointment with Vicki Carmichael, an up-and-coming country music star. *Inside Nashvegas* called her the next Carrie Underwood.

"I'll only be gone a couple of years. The absence will make our hearts grow fonder." Cami gave her sister a teasing smile.

"Promise me you'll get a social life in Indianapolis."

"If social life means work, work, work, then yes, I promise."

"I'm never going to be a matron of honor at your wedding, am I?"

Cami laughed. "I don't know, how matronly do you want to be?"

"Less than a hundred, if you don't mind."

"Then ninety-nine it is."

Cami didn't want to confess that one hunky man had been on her mind all week. Ben Carter. From how he looked without his shirt—downright drool-worthy—to how real and down-to-earth he'd been. How he seemed to really care about the inn even though he had an incredible job waiting for him in Sydney. Viridian resorts were extraordinary. Staying at one was on her bucket list.

Meanwhile, this Wednesday marked a week since she'd given Ben the forty-eight-hour deadline.

You have forty-eight hours.

She cringed at the memory. Please. The deadline had made her sound like a henchman in *The Godfather*. Made her sound like a bully. She never gave potential sellers that kind of rush. But she'd been emotional and mixed-up after seeing Mama's painting, after all the memories.

Ben's delayed response had given her time to think and

plan. She had to go back to Hearts Bend and win him over. Then she'd remembered the flyer about a barn dance on the bulletin board outside the inn's kitchen. After a quick shopping trip last night, she was ready to do-si-do in a lace dress and pair of leather cowboy boots.

She'd wanted to use this drive to the wedding venue to tell Annalise about the inn, but it suddenly felt personal. Talking about business was easy. But talking about the pieces of her heart that touched on her memories of Mama often seemed impossible.

"What about you, Lise? You feeling okay? You look puny."

"I'm fine. We ate sushi last night, and it didn't sit well with me."

"You hate sushi."

"Exactly."

Cami squeezed her sister's hand. "All right, tell me more about Vicki's wedding so far, without all the ideas and changes. What's her theme?"

"She loves color. Wants lots of flowers and eclectic table settings. She loves antiques, yet she sends me pictures of modern weddings with gold-and-white themes. I can't talk to anyone about anything without making them sign a non-disclosure. One will be included in all the wedding invitations. It must be signed when they return their RSVP."

"Remind me to never envy the rich and famous."

"Which reminds me, you'll have to sign this"—Annalise reached into her bag and pulled out a folded legal document —"before we go in."

"You mean I can't take a bunch of pictures and post on social media?"

Annalise laughed. "No."

In Cami's eyes, her sister still looked tired and a bit green. The BMW's GPS told Cami to take the exit on the right. Well, if she was going to tell her sister about the inn and Ben, now was the time. They'd arrive at the venue about the time Annalise dug in for the deep, personal questions.

"I put an offer on the Hearts Bend Inn." Cami gripped the wheel, waiting for her sister's response.

"You what?" Annalise pressed her hand on Cami's arm. "Does Dad know?"

"He will. It's in the system, but I've not closed yet."

"You really want to go back there, Cami? Why?" Annalise's questions mirrored Cami's. Especially *why*.

After her big show-off last week, the *why* question had begun to surface. Why would she want to own the place where her mother died? The place her father hated. The place where words had been exchanged.

"Jean Carter died, and her grandson, Ben, inherited it. Keith Niven emailed and said Ben might be willing to sell. Ben works for Viridian Jewel Resorts and—"

"Ben? Your first-kiss Ben?" Now Annalise teased her. "Is he still cute?"

"No, he's a downright hunk. *Really* handsome. He's opening a marquee hotel in Sydney, and he has to be there the same time I have to be in Indy."

"Do you think he'll sell? I mean, the Carters owned that place since the late '50s. And I think they inherited from someone in the family. It's a legacy."

"He's not sure. He's considering my offer. The place needs a lot of work. A local businessman, Frank Hardy, offered to buy it for the amount of the bank loan, but that was an insulting offer. You know him. He's Sam Hardy's dad."

"Oh, I know Sam Hardy. Steve yells at him every Sunday afternoon in the fall." Annalise lowered her voice. "'Good grief, Hardy, I can pass better than that.'" Steve was a huge Tennessee Titans fan. "So, if Ben says yes, what will Akron do with a small-town inn? Doesn't seem like one of your usual properties." Annalise shifted in the passenger seat. "Frankly, I'm surprised you're even considering this. I thought you'd never go there again. I know Dad won't."

Which was probably a good thing. Cami could oversee everything about the property.

For now, she took the exit and merged onto 41A, still heading north. Traffic was lighter and she sailed through a few green lights.

"Cami, are you going to answer my question? Why do you want to own the Hearts Bend Inn?"

"Well, I wasn't really sure until now, but something hit me when I read Keith's email. Maybe I should go back, touch base with the last place I saw Mama. It's been fifteen years. I've healed. Some. It felt good to walk the grounds with Ben. See the places I used to paint with Mama."

"Did you go to Cottage Three?"

"No, but I don't have to deal with Cottage Three if I—if Akron owns the inn. Did you know she left a painting in the lobby? It was a gift for Dad, but she died before she could give it to him, so he left it there."

"Gosh, no. But I'm not surprised. Dad...he's never really dealt with the grief. He covers up all his pain with bitterness."

"I want the inn to be my own project. Akron has to change with the times, and since I'll be in charge someday, I'll try a few things now. The inn is chump change compared to what we normally do. I made an offer, and to be honest, I think Ben's going to take it."

"Don't be surprised at Dad's reaction, Cami. He hates that place more than you."

"I don't hate that place. Not anymore." Tears threatened at the thought of what had become of her relationship with Dad.

"Maybe I'm being a Pollyanna, but I hope one day the inn will remind him of who he used to be."

"He doesn't want to be reminded, Cami." Annalise had never had the tension with Dad Cami had had after Mama died. But then again, she hadn't been there when it all went down.

The Cumberland Oasis came into view, and Cami slowed to turn in. "When I showed up, Ben asked me if I'd come for the painting. I didn't even know what he was talking about."

"You don't have to buy the whole inn to get the painting, Cami."

"That's just it, Annalise. I think I do."

"So you think Ben's going to sell? If I know you, you have a plan to win him over."

"Saturday night I'm going to the Hearts Bend square dance."

"How do you know he's going to be there?"

"If he's not, I'll go to the inn. Show I'm not in it just for the property but that I care about the town as well as the inn."

"Do you?" Annalise sounded dubious.

"Yes, I think I do."

"All right, then I want pictures. You at a square dance? Can't see it." Annalise's laugh floated through the car. "Time-stamped photos to prove you're there *all* night. And several with Ben. I'm curious what he looks like now."

"You're on. And by the end of the night, Ben Carter will agree to sell me Hearts Bend Inn."

CHAPTER 5

*S*he was a city girl in a country venue and completely out of her comfort zone. Skilled dancers swung about the barn floor to the directions of skilled callers.

Cami had no idea how to allemande left and felt sure if she tried, her leather cowboy boots would betray her feet.

Coyly scanning the dance floor and barn perimeter, she looked for Ben but saw no sign of him. The concession line ran along the back wall advertising cheese and nachos, hot dogs, chips, sodas, popcorn, and ice-cream bars.

A band supported the caller, and as one dance ended, another began. The place was packed—and hot. Large fans anchored in the four corners swung from side to side, stirring the hot air but doing nothing to really cool the space.

Cami pulled out her phone and snapped a selfie at the entrance of the community barn with a bunch of folks gathered behind her. She took another at the snack stand, still looking for Ben. Or Myrtle May.

She was about to take another selfie in front of the band when someone plucked her phone from her hand.

"Hey—" But the protest died when laughing blue eyes of an incredibly good-looking man captivated her. Ben.

His short reddish-blond hair was perfectly messed, and his stubble, almost a beard now, cut close to his angular jaw. The plaid shirt showcased his wide shoulders, and his jeans fit just right.

"What are you doing here?" Ben added a Southern drawl, which sent a slight thrill through her. "I don't think you came all the way to Hearts Bend to take selfies at a square dance."

"Hello to you too." Cami held up her hand. "Phone please. I'm proving to my sister that I'm here."

"So, why are you here?"

"Convincing you to sell me the inn."

He laughed. "You might try adding a few dollars to your offer." He looked at her boots. "Then you wouldn't have to wear those ridiculous things."

"Hey, leave my shoes out of it. These are legit cowboy boots and completely appropriate for tonight." But he was right. So very right. "And I might consider upping the offer. What do you say to—"

"I don't do business at a barn dance." Ben handed over her phone and grabbed her hand, dragging her to the dance floor.

"Ben, seriously, I do not know how to square dance. I'll step all over your toes."

But he wasn't listening. He'd just lined them up with the twirling couples when the caller ended the dance and announced a short break.

Then, from the suspended speakers, a slow song began to play, and Luke Bryan sang about the girl he used to know. One by one, couples gathered in a slow, close sway.

Ben pulled Cami close, and she did absolutely nothing to resist him. His embrace was warm, strong, and oh-so-amazing.

"I thought this was a square dance," she whispered, her lips close to his ear.

"I'm leading you in the box step." His voice tickled her ear as he leaned closer, his breath against her ear. "That's a square."

She muffled her laugh against his shoulder. Then she stepped on his toe. "Oh, Ben, I'm so—"

"Just dance, Cami. Feel." He held her closer. "Don't over-think it. Follow my lead. The box step is easy as pie."

"Cherry or pecan?"

"Apple."

"Hmm. Not my favorite, but..."

One slow song led to another. She quickly relaxed into his arms and found her rhythm. Following his steps was easy. His cheek brushed hers, and the hair of his beard tickled her in a delicious way. She could get used to this.

"How do you normally spend your Friday nights, then, Cami?"

"Working, then takeout followed by a soak in my tub, music in the background." Annalise was right, and it was time to get a life outside of work. "What about you, Ben? How do you normally spend your Friday nights?"

He chuckled and Cami leaned back to study his face. He probably spent his Friday nights with pretty girls in trendy restaurants.

"Working, so I can't bust you for it."

"Birds of a feather and all that."

Just when she was feeling like she never wanted to leave his arms, the band returned, and Ben roped her into square dancing.

She eventually got the hang of it. Dancing with Ben was fun. She couldn't help but laugh as she do-si-doed around him.

On the last note of the song, Ben wrapped an arm around

her waist, pulled her close. She whipped out her phone. "Proof we danced. Annalise isn't going to believe it."

"You need video footage too. Hey, Ray!" Ben waved over an older gentleman in denim overalls and wearing a floppy fisherman's hat. "Cami, you remember the gardener, right?"

She did. Ray had brought in special flowers just for Mama to paint. During that last summer, he'd even planted camellias for Cami to paint. Another memory she'd locked away.

"Ray, do you remember Cami Jackson?"

"Macie's little girl? Sure do. You're all grown up. Saw you at the inn not too long ago."

Cami nodded, but before she could respond, Ben held up Cami's phone. "Cami would like a video of one dance. Could you dance with her while I take it?"

Ray shook his head. "As much as it pains me to turn a pretty girl down, why don't I video and you dance?"

Ben handed the phone to Ray, and as the next song started, Ben and Cami hurried to join the line, hand in hand.

Cami laughed through the song with Ben purposefully missing steps and throwing her off beat. When was the last time she'd had so much fun?

Ray handed back her phone when the dance ended, but Ben quickly reached for it.

"Hey, Ben Carter, hand over my phone." Cami tried to snatch it away, but Ben held it over his head.

"Let's find a place to cool off." He grabbed her hand. "Pie and ice cream at Ella's?"

"Oh my gosh, I love Ella's." She tried for her phone again, but he tucked it in his pocket.

"Care to walk? It's not far." His hand still held hers.

"Sure, I'd love to walk."

Myrtle May deserved a thank-you of epic proportions. Ben would never have gone to the square dance tonight if not for her prompting. And now he was going to enjoy dessert at Ella's.

Come on, it'll be fun. You know what they say: all work and no play makes Ben a very dull boy.

Dull? He was dull, wasn't he? He felt it. Working the inn during the day and Sydney by night. But because of Myrtle May's nagging, tonight he'd danced with the prettiest girl in attendance—Cami Jackson. She'd looked like a million bucks when she walked into the barn, long dark hair in curls down her back, a lace dress, denim jacket, and expensive-looking cowboy boots.

"Are you ever going to return my phone?" Cami said as he held Ella's door for her, resting his hand on the small of her back as she passed.

"Maybe."

As they'd strolled across the moonlit park, the cool breeze against their faces, she'd stayed close, her hand fitting perfectly in his. He was enveloped in the magic of Hearts Bend, and he'd keep her phone forever to stay in this moment.

Inside Ella's, they chose a booth by the windows. A girl played guitar on a small corner stage, and several older couples sat at tables, laughing and talking. Ben passed Cami a menu, and they talked over their options. He ordered apple pie à la mode and iced tea. She ordered cherry à la mode and sweet tea.

"I've eaten pie all over the world. Ella's is the best." Ben slid Cami's phone across the table. "Did you really come tonight to talk me into selling?"

"Yes, but I've had so much fun, I'm not sure I want to talk business." She held her phone in her hand, then tucked it into her pocket. "Tonight reminded me there's more to life than work."

"Me too. I forget to have fun sometimes. So, what about my

forty-eight-hour window?" He mimicked Marlon Brando's *The Godfather.*

"Ugh, don't remind me." Cami laughed softly. "I sounded so stupid. I never give a client a deadline."

"You're a businesswoman. Deadlines are a natural part of offers."

"Not for me and not like that. Anyway, when Keith Niven emailed me about the inn, thinking it might be for sale, I'd just learned I was moving to Indianapolis. I think I felt suddenly sentimental."

"You weren't part of the Indy planning?"

"No, but that's the way it rolls with Brant Jackson." Cami sipped her sweet tea. "He dangled vice president in front of me and I bit. Since you didn't answer me in forty-eight hours..." She smiled. "I've been asking myself why I made the offer. Do I really want to own an inn? It's too small for Akron to manage, so I'd have to do it on my own. Can I do that from Indy?"

"Believe it or not, I'm right there with you, right down to the sentiment. But how can I put my career on hold for a few sentimental feelings and old memories? The memories are with me whether I own the inn or not."

"But it's also your family heritage."

"Weren't you the one who told me my grandparents' work didn't have to be mine?"

"Yeah, don't quote me my wisdom when I don't want to hear it." She was so pretty when she smiled. "But several times this week, it felt like the inn was my heritage. Yet I didn't grow up here like you."

"You spent a lot of summers here. That counts." Ben gulped his tea, still trying to cool off from the hot barn. "Funny how we're debating our sentiments over brick and mortar and a patch of dirt. Life isn't in things, is it?"

"No, but things make us feel connected to people. To the

past."

The waitress came around with their pie and ice cream. "Tina popped in to get something, saw you two and said it's on the house. Said she's sorry about your granny, Ben. You're Ben, right?"

"I am. Tell her thanks"—he checked her name tag—"Alice."

Cami took her first bite of warm pie and cold ice cream. She closed her eyes, and Ben watched her savor the flavors, then glanced away, feeling there was something oddly intimate about the moment.

"Maybe that's what we're debating, Ben. This. Free pie and ice cream because the owner of the local diner recognized you and offered it on the house. You don't get that at a Viridian Jewel Resorts property unless you're in the millionaire's suite dropping ten thousand or more a day."

"Connection," Ben said, more from his heart than his head.

"Connection," she echoed. "Maybe that's why I'm here."

They sat in comfortable silence, eating, sipping their tea. He'd have a sugar hangover tomorrow, but it'd be worth it. The waitress returned for refills, and Cami switched to water. Then as if on some cosmic cue, she asked for a helping of fries as the exact same words left Ben's lips.

"Two orders of fries coming up," Alice said. "Look, you want anything else? Tina said it's all on the house."

"No," Ben said. "Fries are enough." Cami agreed.

"All right, Ben Carter, tell me about you. When I last saw you, we were fifteen going on sixteen, heading into tenth grade."

"Nothing exciting. Graduated from Rock Mill High. Went to University of Tennessee, which you know. Go Vols. Then I went to stay with Mom and Dad in Papua New Guinea. I'd felt disconnected from them for a long time, so I thought I'd help out in their ministry. They have a great team, Americans and locals, working with them, and I felt more in the way than anything."

"I'm sure you were a big help."

"It was good to be with the folks. But missionary life was never for me. The week before I came back here, a typhoon came through. Then it was all hands to the pump. People came from all over the world to dig people out from under mud and fallen structures. I felt useful then. One of the volunteers was from the Turquoise—the Viridian Jewel resort in New Zealand. He was impressed with my work ethic and offered me a job. Seven years later, I've opened and managed five VJ resorts, with my biggest job on the horizon—launching a marquee hotel."

"What location was your favorite?"

He thought for a moment, stifled by a grip of emotion. Hearts Bend Inn was his favorite. No place like home...

"Budapest. Manhattan was fun too."

Alice brought a very large plate of hot, steamy fries with a side of chili cheese for dipping.

Cami opened a fresh napkin roll. "I'm going to gain five pounds tonight."

"After all that square dancing, you earned it."

She raised her hand for a fist bump.

"What about you?" he said. "How'd you get into Akron Development? I figured you to be an artist, selling your prints at Nashville's top galleries."

"Art doesn't pay the bills. Or buy my shoes." She laughed. "Minus the typhoon and living in a foreign country, my story is a lot like yours. After Mama died, life sort of fell apart. I lost interest in painting. Mama was my mentor, my..."

"Muse?" Ben said.

"Yes. She was my muse. Dad buried himself in work. Annalise was busy with college, and even though she hovered, I was still on my own. Got into a bit of trouble—nothing serious. Pulled a Ferris Bueller, then decided I didn't want to be a girl who messed up her life because something bad happened. Mama wouldn't like it. As you know, I went to University of Georgia. Go Dawgs." Ben made a gagging face. She grinned. "Majored in finance with a double minor in business and art. Graduated with honors. I worked for Akron in the summers as an intern. Believe you me, I didn't have any privilege or favor. I had to apply for the internships like everyone else."

"I have to respect that, but you'd think your dad would give you a bit of a break."

"You'd think." She munched on a fry dipped in chili cheese. "I think I just wanted to connect to him. In my mind, he replaced Mama as my mentor. If he said, 'Apply,' I did. He says, 'Go to Indy.' I say, 'When do I leave?'"

He felt for her, understanding the journey of trying to be acceptable to one's parents. He'd been there with his own.

They polished off the fries over a rowdy discussion of college sports, mainly football, which morphed into an exchange on how to manage staff.

"Make them feel like they have something to contribute," Ben said.

"I give rewards. You work hard for me, I'll show my appreciation."

Cami drained her water and shoved the glass aside. Ben did the same with his sweet tea, leaning toward her, arms on the blue-and-gold Formica table. She looked like she had something to say.

"What about my offer? Still a no-go?"

"Your mom died there, Cami. You haven't been back in, what, fifteen years? I want to know the deep-down reason you want it."

She sighed and looked away, then brushed a tear from

under her eye. "You just said it. Because Mama died there, Ben. I guess it's my way of memorializing her." Her eyes brimmed when she looked at him. "I'm figuring this out as we go. Following my gut."

Oh man, what was she doing to him? She was making him want to sell. But if he did, shouldn't he get top dollar as a memorial of his grandparents? Shouldn't he have a chunk of change to give Dad, Mom, and Myrtle May? He'd need top dollar, and right here, right now, he wasn't sure nine hundred thousand was top dollar.

The inn, with some investment, could be a fantastic destination place. But he'd not had time to research the value without renovations.

His parents had given their lives to God and the mission field. Now it was up to Ben to make sure they were set for the end of their lives. He was all they had.

"We've said all sentiment aside, right?" he said. "If I sell, I want top dollar. This is my grandparents' legacy, and I want to set up my parents for retirement. I need to settle the inn's debt. Make sure MM is set. Give Walt and Ray something for their retirement. They're like family."

A tear drifted to the edge of Cami's eye. She grinned as she dabbed it away. "I hear you, but I'm still a skilled Akron negotiator, Ben Carter. If you sell to me, it'll be for bottom dollar. The place needs a lot of work. I respect what you want to do with the money, but my offer is fair. Maybe more than fair. Tell you what, I'll cover the bank loan and still sell at nine hundred thousand."

Now she was just showing off. "You're making it hard to say no. But can you promise Akron won't tear it down?"

"That's my father's way. Not mine."

"So, of all the properties you've acquired, none of them have been bulldozed."

Cami sat back with a hot glint in her eye. The sentiment of tears vanished. "Sometimes we sell them to other developers. Sometimes they get torn down for new projects. Ben, I promise, the inn will not be torn down."

"Once you go to Indy, it's perfectly plausible your dad could sell the inn out from under you. Frank Hardy probably won't go away. Or a new developer will come in, buy it for the land and location and tear it down, put up an office building or open a sub shop."

"I'll make sure he doesn't."

"Didn't he just send you to Indianapolis without even discussing it with you?" He was turning into the man who negotiated contracts with foreigners and navigated cultural differences. The Hearts Bend boy was now a shadow.

"Ben, if you don't want to sell to me, don't. You can't keep challenging me. But let me ask you. How are you going to pay the bank?"

"There are ways. Refinance. Find investors." Had he just made his decision?

"Okay, what about building the business? You have to grow to stay solvent. What about taxes, insurance, payroll? You'll have to hire a manager to run things if you're in Sydney or Hong Kong."

She was pushing. And he didn't like to be pushed. "If you want it so much, up your offer."

"I just did."

"Try again."

Her cheeks flashed red. "And if I don't?"

"I'll keep it."

"So, you're turning my offer down?"

"Yeah, Cami, for the second time, I think I am."

And for about sixty seconds, he knew he'd done the exact right thing.

CHAPTER 6

*B*y Wednesday, Ben was buried under work. Last Friday night with Cami seemed ages ago.

He woke up every morning to a mountain of overnight emails from Jordan and a field of messages from Jim about Sydney, Hong Kong, and begging him to return to Sydney.

In the afternoon, he worked inn issues. Repairing porch boards, weeding the gardens, setting up to paint the cottages. Ray worked along with him some days, other days he took on separate projects. All the while, Ben's doubts mounted.

How was he going to keep this place?

By Friday afternoon, he regretted turning Cami down. He picked up his phone several times to call her but never dialed. Something held him back.

He loved this place, warts and all. But quitting his job to run Hearts Bend Inn simply was not an option. He'd signed a contract with VJR. The success of the Emerald rested squarely on his shoulders. Jim was right. Ben needed to be in Sydney.

If he walked out on Viridian in the middle of launching a

marquee property, he'd never work in the industry again. Not at that level anyway.

Mr. Graham popped by one afternoon to say he'd talked to Stan at the bank about a refinance. Stan seemed reluctant but he might be willing to talk.

A refi would buy Ben a bit more time, but he'd still have to keep the inn running from Sydney to make the payments. With the Fourth of July coming up, he'd hoped to see more reservations, but so far, only half the rooms were booked.

Had word got around the place was falling apart? Frank Hardy, maybe? Or Akron. Brant, not Cami. Ben didn't think that sort of thing was her style.

As he headed out to the barn to search for paint brushes, he replayed last Friday night in his mind. Dancing with Cami. Sharing pie and fries with Cami. Laughing with Cami. Talking with Cami. She was the same girl he'd known all those years ago. Until they'd ended up talking business, anyway.

Another time, another place, he'd pursue her till she couldn't resist. He could love her. He had when he was a teen. But this was not the right time or place. He'd be in Sydney by September first. She'd be in Indy. Worlds and time zones apart.

Still, images of her crept past his mind's eye while he worked, while he slept. If he paused even for a minute to remember, he could feel her chin on his shoulder, the warmth of her palm in his as they danced. The sweet scent of her floral perfume.

Ben stepped into the stale, hot atmosphere of the inn's barn. He shoved the door all the way open for fresh air and light. The barn was a world all its own, stuffed with bins, cans and boxes, treasures, and—he hoped—paint brushes. He'd looked in the shed first but hadn't seen any.

This week, he'd repaired the doors on the inn and the shutters and doors on the cottages. They really needed to be replaced, but for now, a bit of paint would pretty them up.

Ben scanned the boxes on the metal shelves, many of them labeled with Granddaddy's handwriting. Some with Ray's. Some had no label at all. He suspected those had arrived here during Granny's reign.

Paint brushes, paint brushes. Where would they be? He reached up for a box marked brushes, tipping the metal casing forward just enough to send a can of old doorknobs to the concrete floor.

"Have mercy, are you trying to wake the dead?" Ben looked up to see Ray at the barn door, his ever-present fisherman's hat on his head. He pulled a white hanky out of his shirt pocket and mopped his forehead. "There's a fan in here somewhere."

"I'm looking for the paint brushes." Ben stooped to collect the knobs. Good to know these were out here in case he couldn't replace a broken one from the inn. "Did you test the pond water?"

"Yeah, the alkaline levels were fine, but I'll keep an eye on it." Ray pulled a large industrial fan from the corner and plugged it in to one of the sockets attached to the workbench.

The motor kicked in and the blades whirred. Darn thing nearly blew Ben into the back wall.

"I'll turn it down some," Ray said. "Now, what do you need?"

"Paint brushes."

"The brushes are in the shed. Those boxes where you're looking hold a mix of things." Ray walked over, reached up, and touched an unmarked box. "Extension cords. This one has the doodads your Granny let the wedding photographer keep on premise."

"Wedding photographer?" Ben set the can of doorknobs back on the shelf.

"There's even more in that large container in the back corner."

"How long has it been since we had a wedding here?" More than a couple of minutes, for sure.

"Jean hoped to have weddings and receptions again. But when the Wedding Chapel opened, brides took their business there. When the Wedding Shop opened their doors again, Jean thought the wedding business would return to Hearts Bend, but nothing much came of it. Brides loved the chapel but took their receptions to fancier places than the inn." Ray tipped his hat back. "Guess we just got too old and run-down looking. But your Granny held onto hope. She always was a dreamer."

Ben twisted away from a flash of guilt. He'd had no idea Granny hadn't stopped hosting weddings by choice. He'd figured she'd just lost interest.

But Ray was right. The inn was not in the kind of pristine condition that attracted a bride and her mother.

However, weddings and receptions were the least of his worries. He needed paint brushes.

"So, you and the Jackson girl..." Ray leaned against one of the shelves, arms folded, the fan humming in the background.

"Don't get any ideas, Ray. She only wants to buy the inn."

"Does she now?"

"I turned her down."

Ray made a face and nodded. "You got a plan besides painting old shutters and doors?"

"Not really. No." Which doubled his irritation. Since he'd joined VJR, he'd planned his life. This indecisiveness sat hard with him.

Sell. Just do it. He didn't have *time* for sentiment.

"You know if you sell to Cami, her Daddy will come knock the place down."

Ben turned to Ray. "That's what I said, but she promised

he wouldn't. She wants to preserve her mother's memory. But if I sell, am I desecrating my *grandparents'* memory? My own memories?"

"Funny thing about memories," Ray said. "You can't trust them. Can't use them to plug up your fears. Or make you do something you don't want to do."

Wise words from the old groundskeeper. "Is that what I'm doing? Letting my memories hold me back?"

"Seems to me Cami's trying to reclaim something she lost too. You must live your life, Ben. Not someone else's. Besides, memories aren't stuck inside buildings, they're kept in here." Ray tapped his chest and started for the door. "I'll get the brushes for you. Then I'm going to the hardware store. The motor on the pond windmill broke."

He was right. One hundred percent. Ben's life before Granny died had been fancy hotels in world-class cities. His father, who should've inherited the inn, was running a major missions program that ministered to thousands of people. He certainly wasn't coming back to run the family business.

Walking out of the barn into the bright sunlight, Ben pulled his phone from his pocket and looked at Cami's name. Did he call? Did he let go of the inn? What did she really want from it?

Could he trust her?

His phone rang. Jim. Well, at least he didn't have to figure it out right now, because Sydney was calling.

Again.

Saturdays were meant for relaxing, not tapping your fingers on the table of the local coffee shop. Already, Cami had looked through all the listings Max, the Realtor in Indy, had sent—nothing made her want to pack up her life and hang a Home

Sweet Home sign. She drank a latte and ate a cinnamon roll, and it was only nine. Marta had showings lined up in Cami's condo all day and had requested she be out an hour ago.

Right now, someone was walking through her place, the one she'd worked so hard to buy and build out the way she wanted.

Did she really want to sell? Maybe she could lease it. She texted Marta with the idea, then sat back and looked toward the street and the start of a beautiful day.

Across the room, a couple sat at one of the tables. They looked happy. In love. Would she ever find love? Real love? She'd not been on a date in—

She had to stop and think. Do a bit of math. Three years? Good grief.

She picked up her empty coffee cup. She shouldn't order another. But she couldn't sit here much longer while strangers walked through her condo either. Yesterday she'd had lunch with Annalise, who'd talked of nothing but the Vicki Carmichael wedding. Cami hadn't gotten a word in edgewise. Annalise had still looked a little green around the gills, but her sister was a big girl and said she was fine. Cami would respect that. For now.

Which meant she had to steer clear of Annalise today. She'd be eyeball-deep in wedding planning details. So that was a definite no-go.

As she cleaned off her table and packed up her laptop, Marta texted.

The first couple went wild over the place. They'll probably put in an offer above asking. #exciting

Oh great. Did you see my text about leasing?

Cami waited a few beats, but Marta didn't respond. Okay, she was busy. But Cami would get an answer sooner or later.

The truth of the matter was, as the move to Indy became

more of a reality, Cami was growing anxious. Yes, she was excited to head up an Akron expansion office, but she mourned leaving Nashville. She mourned leaving her sister and brother-in-law. Even mourned leaving Dad. How would the distance impact their relationship?

Mourned that she hadn't gotten the inn. She'd called Annalise Monday evening to talk it out.

"I wasn't sure how I felt about the inn until Ben said no. Then I was really disappointed."

"You have a lot of Mom memories there. More than I do."

"I felt close to her when I was there. I didn't realize until now. I'm not sad about it being the place where she died; I'm excited to be on the grounds of the place she loved so much. She always wanted Dad to buy it."

"Like the Carters would ever let it go."

"I feel like I've let her down again."

"Oh, Cami, no. She'd be so proud of you. Promise."

"At least one parent is proud." Cami had laughed and taken it back before Annalise could launch into her lecture of how Cami had Dad all wrong.

No, Annalise had Dad all wrong. At least when it came to Cami.

Heading to the car, Cami set her purse in the back seat. She could shop, see if there were any shoes needing a good home.

However, instead of heading to the Green Hills Mall, she hopped on I-440 to I-40 and aimed for Hearts Bend. A memory flashed of Mom taking her to Haven's Bakery for hot donuts and hot chocolate. Sweet sugar, cinnamon, chocolate—she could practically smell the bakery in her car.

The moment she crossed under the *Welcome to Hearts Bend* sign, a weight lifted off her. Slowing down for the first of HB's two stop lights, she opened the sunroof and decided on a quick stop at Java Jane's.

What was Ben doing? Did he like iced latte? If not, she'd drink his.

Ten minutes later she pulled into the inn's empty parking lot. The grounds were quiet as she headed toward the inn with a Java Jane's caddy. Where were the guests?

The lobby was equally as barren as the lot except for Bart, who click-clacked his way toward her, tail wagging.

"Hey, buddy, did they leave you to man the front desk?" The dog wagged his tail faster as she ran her hand over his head and around his ears. "Ben? Myrtle May?"

The silence of the lobby surrounded her. The midday sunlight splashed through the windows and across the hardwood, playing peek-a-boo with the few clouds in the sky. Suddenly the light shifted as a cloud blocked the sun. A shadow mysteriously crept up the wall to Mom's pastoral painting.

Cami stepped closer, memories, feelings stirring, knocking, demanding her attention.

For a moment, she lived in the serene scene, young, innocent, full of hope, in the arms of a man she loved.

Mom's expert brushstrokes were thick and bold in the field and trees, yet delicate and light for the couple sitting on the bench.

An artist's brushstroke distinguished her, like her handwriting or the sound of her voice. Mom's brush showed her confidence. Her ability to love and... Cami lightly touched the head of the couple. Forgive.

She battled a hot flash of tears just as a crash came from the kitchen. Raised voices followed. Bart curled in his bed with a bark.

"Listen here, Walt. I said there was no reason to take offense. I'm just saying, no one wants onions for breakfast."

"Who says? I love onions in my omelets *and* my tuna."

"Do you now? I suppose that's why you ain't been kissed since Reagan was president."

"Listen here, woman—"

Cami checked her laugh as Myrtle May burst through the kitchen door wearing a red top with yellow sequins in the shape of sunflowers, purple slacks, and brown, sensible sandals. Bart bounded from the bed to greet her by burying his nose against her leg.

"Cami, goodness, when did you arrive?" Myrtle May pressed her hand to her chest, a bit flustered, then took her chair at the desk.

"Just now." Cami backed away from the painting, from the memories of Mama's sweet voice, her gentle hand on Cami's shoulder as she whispered encouragement in her ear and held up the caddy. "I was looking for Ben."

"He's out by the cottages." Myrtle May smiled, then pointed toward the kitchen. "I suppose you heard all that?"

"Heard all of what?" Cami winked and headed for the door. Maybe she was seeing things, but Myrtle May looked a bit flushed.

Out on the porch, Cami looked in the direction of the cottages. Was he in Cottage Three? The one where she and Mom always stayed. The one where—

Cami squared her shoulders, raised her chin, and breathed deep. Maybe it was good she wasn't buying the inn. She'd not have to deal with those memories.

She found Ben outside of Cottage One working on the siding. He wore his Titans hat backward, jeans, and a sweat-soaked T-shirt. When he stood, she felt that rush again from the day she'd caught him sawing the tree.

"Ding-dong," she said, holding up the lattes. "Cami-Dash. Your iced latte is here."

"Hey, wow, thanks." He set the hammer in his toolbox,

wiped his brow with a towel, and reached for one of the cups. "What brings you out this way?"

"There are showings in my condo all day, and I was feeling a bit restless." She sipped her iced latte. "Ah. Perfection in a cup."

Ben set his cup down next to the toolbox. "If you have a mind to help out while I finish this siding, it will go faster, then we can grab a pizza."

"You don't want to grab lunch here?"

"Are you kidding? Walt is making tuna. On a weekend. Myrtle May is fit to be tied. Let's get as far away as possible."

"You're on. Tell me what to do."

CHAPTER 7

*T*his sort of thing required a celebration. Ben had finished the siding, and he'd spent time with Cami Jackson.

It still boggled his mind that she'd showed up. Maybe this was God's way of telling him to sell, assuming God was interested in the inn. Or interested in Ben.

Ben opened the door to the pizzeria for Cami. Dimmed lights, soft music, flickering candles—it was the perfect mix for romance.

He chose a table near the front, but Cami moved to the back corner. A booth where he was sure couples liked to hide, sneak kisses.

"Is this okay? I like sitting in a booth." Her smile was innocent and sweet. Of course, he agreed.

Cami reached for a menu. "This place smells amazing. Cheese, tomato sauce, pepperoni." She set her menu back. "I'm having pizza."

"Want to share a large New York pepperoni?" Ben said.

"You know it."

The waitress set down a basket of garlic knots and took their drink orders: a root beer for him and a sweet tea for Cami. He ordered their pizza. With extra pepperoni.

Cami passed out the small plates, and they each chose a garlic knot.

"So, tell me, Ms. Jackson, you still interested in the inn?"

"More than anything. I've been thinking how it's a resting place. A place for artists to come and imagine, paint, sculpt, whatever. It doesn't matter, though, because you're not selling. At least, not to me."

To be honest, he didn't know what he was doing, but best to let the conversation die. Right on time, the pizza arrived, and the goodness of Angelo's pizza took over. He and Cami talked current events and business, touched on politics for a few seconds, then it was her turn to get personal.

"Is there a beautiful woman beside the successful hotelier, Ben?"

"No. I dated someone when I lived in Manhattan, but she was a New Yorker, and I was a Southerner."

"And never the two shall meet?"

He laughed. "She had her career, I had mine."

"Do you think about it? Settling down, getting married?"

"If I could have what my grandparents had, yes. But the world is a different place." He took a final bite of his slice, washed it down with root beer, and turned the tables. "What about you? Is there a handsome guy beside the successful property developer?"

"No. But if I could have what my parents had when I was young, yes. Not what they turned into when they grew apart. He worked. They fought. She left him to paint at the inn. She said it was her quiet place."

"Granddaddy used to say, 'Marriage is simple. All you have to do is serve the other and not be selfish.'"

She laughed. "Oh, is that all?"

"Okay, Cami, come on. I'm sitting across from you." Ben tossed his napkin on the table and leaned toward her. "I know what I see. Don't tell me you don't have guys giving you their number or asking for yours."

"Not really. The last guy I dated was three years ago, and we only went out a handful of times."

"You're intimidating, Cami. Beautiful. Smart. Successful. Confident."

"Do I intimidate you?"

"Right down to my boots."

"You are so full of it, Ben Carter." The candlelight haloed her high cheeks and made her eyes bright. "And I'm not confident. I'm just terrified to fail."

"We all fail. You get back up and try again."

"Not if you're the daughter of Brant Jackson. If you fail, it costs a life."

"Costs a life? What are you talking about?"

"Nothing. I'm just yakking."

The waitress arrived to refill their drinks, and the moment was lost. Had Cami had a failure that'd nearly cost a life? Surely, she wasn't talking about her mother. Or anyone.

He was about to pay the bill when a string quartet took their place in the corner. When they started playing, the romantic atmosphere increased.

The maître d' rushed about the dining room, urging couples to dance. "You, *signore,* dance with the *bella signora.*" He stepped aside and motioned to the dance floor, where one other couple did a slow sway. "*Per favore.*"

Ben gave Cami a nod toward the floor, and she slipped out of the booth. With her soft hand holding his, nothing else in the world seemed to matter. It was like they were the only two people on the dance floor. The only two people in the world.

The melody of the strings guided each step and sway. Cami inched closer as his arm tightened around her back.

She smelled like the flowers in the inn's gardens, and he remembered a long-ago night on the dock of the pond with fireflies their only light. They'd been thirteen or fourteen, sitting with a good six feet between them, talking about school and friends, about his parents' call to the mission field, about her love of painting.

He'd been more comfortable with her than anyone other than his grandparents. And he was just as comfortable with her now.

The song ended, but they continued to dance. Cami was warm and enticing.

"I think I could do this all afternoon," he whispered.

"Then we should. The real world will come for us tomorrow."

He laughed and leaned to see her face. If he kissed her, he'd sink into something he felt sure he'd never escape from. So he cleared the emotion from his throat and tried to think of something to say.

"So, if you bought the inn, what's your vision? Really. How will you manage it? What will you do with it?"

"I'll have to think, come up with a plan. Last I heard, you turned me down."

"Okay, I'll give you forty-eight hours." He channeled Marlon Brando again with a deep, gravelly voice.

She laughed and gently patted his chest. "Don't remind me of how stupid I sounded." She moved easily with him as the dance continued and the quartet began a new song. "In my mind, the inn has always been a special place. I see artists like Mom set up on the grounds, painting, finding their muse. The place was always more like a refuge, a way to escape the cares of the world."

A refuge. Cami painted the heart of the inn with her words. His grandparents had themselves been a refuge. For Ben. For those in need on a dark, stormy night.

The inn was just the tool they'd used. How was it that Cami, the daughter of the biggest developer in the South, who'd not been to the inn in fifteen years, understood its purpose better than he?

"What?" she said. "You sighed."

"I just realized how brilliant you are," he said, bringing her close and tracing his finger along her jawline. "That's the inn to a T. I'm going to miss you when I go."

"No, you won't. I'll be in Indianapolis, and you'll find some gorgeous sheila to capture your heart."

"Won't you find a nice, handsome Hoosier to capture yours?" He searched her eyes for some sort of answer, but she'd closed the windows to her soul. His, on the other hand, felt wide open.

However, when Cami shifted her stance and rested her cheek on his shoulder, he started to wonder if his heart hadn't always belonged to her. Would always belong to her.

"Hey," he said, his voice husky. "The Fourth of July is next week. HB still does it big at the Scott farm."

"Next to Christmas it was my favorite holiday. Dad and Mama brought us every year when we were little."

"Will you come? Go with me? You can have any room or cottage you want."

"A room. Not a cottage." Ben heard between the lines. Not Cottage Three. "I'll pay for my room." She moved with him as he stepped back and twirled her under his arm, then pulled her close again. "But I'll let you buy me a hot dog at the celebration. Oh, do they still have the tables and tables of homemade desserts?"

"All the pie you can eat. The Fourth of July, then. It's a date."

She rested her head on his shoulder again and whispered, "It's a date."

For a date, the weather was perfect. And Ben was an even better escort.

The Fourth of July arrived on a beautiful hot and humid Saturday. Cami had met Ben at the inn. They'd driven his Granddaddy's old truck across town and parked on the western end of the field.

Ben slung a couple camping chairs over his shoulder. When she stumbled, stubbing her toe on a clump of dirt and grass, he reached for her.

"You all right?" Ben held on to her longer than necessary, but it was nice to have a man catch her when she fell. Woman power and all that aside.

Note to self: Never wear new red-canvas Sperrys to the Scotts' Fourth of July bash. Even if they match your new patriotic shirt.

They followed the music and scent of barbecue to the party, found Myrtle May and Ray reclining and eating under a large maple and camping fly. The large golden retriever curled at their feet happily chewing on a tennis ball.

"Put your chairs there." Myrtle May pointed to a spot on the other side of the folding table. "Walt's gone to set up his cookies at the inn's booth. He has some of those ten percent off two or more nights coupons you wanted printed up. Good thinking, Ben."

"Want to walk around, get some food?" Ben said, taking her hand again.

"You owe me a hot dog."

"Fine, but I'm going for barbecue."

There was food everywhere. Good food. Amazing food. Cami sampled Haven's cookie specialty, the White Chocolate Cookies and Cream Cookie, as well as one of Walt's cinnamon sugar masterpieces.

"Where has this been all my life?" She held it up to Ben as if she'd discovered fine gold.

"In Walt's head."

"You should get him to write down the recipe. You could market this. Make money for the inn and Walt. Seriously."

"Or you could make money for the inn. I'll be in Sydney."

Cami tugged on his arm, drawing him up short. "Are you saying you'll sell me the inn?"

Ben shrugged. "I didn't say that."

"For today, you're not going to Sydney and I'm not moving to Indianapolis, okay?"

"Why? We'll only be disappointed when we face reality tomorrow. In fact, I'm probably going to have to fly down to Sydney in the next week or so."

"And I may have to go up to Indy. But, Ben, we're here now, carefree, not the world changers we hope to be. I've been Cami the businesswoman for so long I've forgotten what it's like to be Cami the girl who likes to have fun and eat barbecue and hot dogs, and—" She glanced toward the roped-off section for the three-legged race. "Run a three-legged race."

She grabbed Ben's hand and tugged him toward the course before he could protest. This could be fun. She was just enough of a competitor—

"Cami, hold up. You want to run in the three-legged race? You have to be on a team. We used to have one for the inn, but—"

"Ben Carter!" A man with a bullhorn and a clipboard

strolled toward them. "Haven's Bakery needs one more pair for their team. Ruby had to drop out. Twisted her ankle."

Good ole Hooley. Hadn't seen him in years. The man never aged. "Hooley, I don't think we should—"

"Yes, we should." Cami tugged on his T-shirt sleeve. "Come on, please."

"Have you ever been in a three-legged race?"

"Not since I was, like, six." She leaned close to him. "But it would be fun."

"I guess we're in."

Hooley wrote on the paper on his clipboard with a number two pencil. "I'll let Chloe and Sam know. All I need now is a team name."

"Inn It to Win It." Cami laughed as Hooley filled in the small box.

"You'll be in the third heat. Best grab a rope and a sack."

Ben retrieved one of each from the pile. "Line up next to me. Press your leg tight against mine. I'll tie us up with the rope, then we can take a quick practice run before stepping into the sack. We have to move and work together or—"

"Ben Carter, thank you so much." A very pretty brunette approached, holding up two white T-shirts identical to the one she wore tied up at her trim waist. "I didn't even know you were in town. Wow, it's good to see you." She leaned in for a hug, then turned to Cami. "Chloe Hardy. Ben and I graduated together."

"Cami Jackson."

"I have two Haven's Bakery three-legged race tees for you. Cami, I don't have any smalls."

"I'll wear whatever you've got."

"Well, my sweet husband—"

Ben leaned close. "Titans quarterback."

Cami made a face. "I know who Sam Hardy is, Ben. I don't live in a cave."

"He ordered large and extra-large for the whole team. Here you go."

Cami slipped on her T-shirt. It was hard to maneuver with her leg tethered to his.

"Win, lose, or draw—have fun. I'm so grateful you volunteered." Chloe bent toward Ben. "Everyone is gunning for Pop's Yer Uncle."

"Do they still win every year?"

"*Every* year. It's time for a new champ."

Chloe ran off to meet her husband, who was more impressive in real life than on the gridiron.

While the Hardys lined up to race in the first heat, Ben and Cami practiced the best form. Arms tight around each other's waists, hips pressed together.

"Once we get a rhythm"—Ben roped his arm around her —"we should be able to fly."

Races went on all day, but each grand heat had its own champion. In this grand heat, number five, Sam and Chloe won the first heat with a team from the Wedding Shop coming in second.

"The top two teams move on to the final heat," Ben said.

Pop's Yer Uncle won heat number two. A team from the kids' theater came in second.

Finally, Hooley called the third heat. "On the line."

Chloe came up to the starting line. "You got this," she said. "Take your time, focus, run together."

"Ready?" Ben glanced at Cami, smiling. "Start with the outside leg."

"On your mark—" Hooley, from the bullhorn.

Cami and Ben leaned forward. Her heart thundered in her chest. Suddenly the bullhorn blasted, and the racers were off.

Ben kept their cadence. "Out. In. Out. In."

Around them, in front of them, couples toppled.

"Sorry, Cole," Ben hollered as he and Cami leapt over one of the downed racers.

"No, you're not," Cole called. "But go, go, go! Beat Pop's!"

Cami wanted to look behind but feared she'd lose her balance. She whispered with Ben as he kept the pace. "Out. In. Out. In."

"Let's go faster," she breathed out.

Ben picked up the tempo, and as the finish line grew closer, Cami could taste their victory. Suddenly, Chloe appeared in their view, jumping and waving her arms.

"Hurry, Pop's is closing in. Go, go, go!"

In four more strides they crossed the finish line. First place.

"You won, you won!" Chloe raced toward them and grabbed them in a winner's hug. "You were amazing."

Cami was catching her breath as she accepted congratulations, still tied to Ben. When the crowd cleared, they plopped to the ground for a rest.

"That was so fun." Was she glowing? She felt like she was glowing.

Chloe handed them each a bottle of water and an "all the treats you want from the Haven's table."

"I don't think I can eat," Cami said after a long drink.

"We can wait until after our final victory."

"Oh really?" She loved the smile in his wide blue eyes. "You're confident, Carter."

"Sure, why not? Time for a new champ in town."

His ball cap had been knocked sideways, and his short hair glistened with sweat. When Cami reached up to straighten his hat, Ben caught her hand and angled toward her.

"Cami."

"Ben?"

He raised his hand to the side of her face. Was he going to kiss her? Her heartbeat kicked up, sure he was going to kiss her. She tipped toward him just as—

"Winners, on the starting line." Hooley and his darn bullhorn.

Cami didn't move. Nor Ben. If he had something to say, or do, she wanted to know.

Hooley blasted the horn right over their heads.

"Let's go, let's go, winners."

Ben smiled at her, then pushed to his feet, offering his hand to her.

Don't forget where we were, Ben.

At the starting line, Ben secured his arm around her, and Cami knew in that moment, if she had her way, she'd never let him go.

But she didn't get her way, did she? She'd learned that when Mom died. Dad sending her to Indiana proved she was not as in control as she liked to believe.

Letting go was the name of her game.

CHAPTER 8

*P*op's Yer Uncle retained their title in the final heat, but Cami and Ben gave them a run for their money. They lost by inches. Ben blamed Cami. She'd been laughing too hard.

"We could've had them, Cami."

"Then you shouldn't make me laugh."

But oh, her laugh was his new favorite sound.

Anyway, they were celebrated, then handed the little tin second-place trophy to Chloe and Haven's with pride and toasted their almost-victory with a tall glass of sweet tea.

Then it was just...being together. They toured the grounds, watched the games, tried a bounce house, and when the sun began to descend, they moved their chairs to the concert area for the evening's show, performed by hometown boy and country great, Buck Mathews.

When Buck played his last song, "America the Beautiful," fireworks exploded in the sky. Ben gripped Cami's hand, proud to be an American, proud to be with this woman. If only for the day. For a few weeks. For this moment.

He felt so at rest; so, so *normal.* When had he lost touch with that feeling?

At one point during the light show finale, Cami laughed, oohed and aahed at each explosion, gripping his arm and holding on tight. When had *that* started feeling so normal? And very much desired.

When the show ended and she released him to fold up their chairs, Ben felt a bit adrift, as if he'd lost a tether to his life. He reached for the chairs and threw their carrying straps over his shoulder.

"Can we do this again tomorrow?" Cami said, bumping against him as they walked toward Myrtle May's camp. "I had so much fun. The food, the light show, the three-legged race. Man, I really wanted to beat Pop's Yer Uncle."

"You were laughing too hard."

"You were killing me with your Pop's smack talk."

"Suddenly the high school athlete I thought I'd left at Rock Mill High found his voice. So next year they're going down." Next year? He'd be in Sydney. Or more likely, Hong Kong.

"That's it! I'm coming back next year and every year." Cami turned to face him, walking backward. "Ben, you should come too!" Her inflection was a "light bulb" moment.

"I was kidding, but come back for the Fourth every year?" Why would he return to Hearts Bend if he sold the inn? Where would he stay? Then again, wouldn't he want to see what had become of the inn?

"Sure, why not? Like a same-time-next-year sort of reunion."

"Unless, of course, you're madly in love and engaged." Were those words for himself or for Cami?

"No time for romance, Ben." Her tone changed. The laughter was gone. "Next year I'll be buried under Indianapolis property acquisitions. Gotta make that money. Make Dad proud."

"You'll have time for fun."

"I haven't done a good job up till now." Cami slowed her steps. "I miss this part of life. Being in a community, going places where people know your name. And not because you're bringing a large check."

"Why not talk your dad into small acquisitions like the inn. Renovate. Take your time with them. Enjoy them."

"He doesn't want to be in the renovation business. But doesn't mean I can't take the risk. I have some latitude with Akron, believe it or not." She walked with him toward the inn's setup, and he could almost feel her warmth. "Akron started with the nickel and dime properties. When Dad got into high-end acquisitions, he quit with the smaller projects. He's brilliant at reading the market, knowing when to adjust. Akron has survived deflation, inflation, market fluxes. While other businesses went under, we stayed on top."

"You sound proud." Ben stopped by Myrtle May and Walt, who seemed deep in quiet conversation. He'd love to know what that was about. "We're heading home. Do y'all need any help?"

Myrtle May waved him off. "Naw, we're good. See you kids in the morning. Are you staying, Cami?"

"No, I need to get back. The Realtor is showing my loft."

Cami's confession struck him with a bit of reality. Don't get caught up in the romance of fireworks and three-legged races. She was moving to Indianapolis. He was due Down Under as soon as possible.

Walking beside him toward the truck, she stumbled over something, a clump of dirt maybe, and Ben grabbed her hand.

"Thanks."

"You're welcome."

But he didn't let go. Her hand felt good in his. She fit as they walked around parked cars and through the shadows of the day.

"Earlier you said I must be proud of my dad, and I am, Ben," she said softly. "He can be hard-nosed. I know Hearts Bend folks don't care much for him, but he's fair and honest."

Ben stopped at the inn's truck and lowered the tailgate, sliding the chairs into the bed.

"You said he's good at reading the market, but is he good at reading you?"

"Whoa, ladies and gentlemen, Ben Carter saw an opportunity and took a shot." Cami laughed softly and bumped his shoulder.

"You don't have to answer."

But he wanted her to answer, to open her heart a bit. Something about the dark made it easy to be vulnerable.

"It's complicated between us, Ben. He loves me. I don't doubt that at all. He's setting me up for a long and prosperous career. He's made me work for it. Doesn't show me favoritism in the workplace, yet he does send me information from his personal emails, details about a transaction and articles on the market, things he doesn't send to the rest of the team. I've been invited to lunches and dinners with investors, bankers, politicians. He's teaching me to be like him."

"But are you? Like him?"

"I am now. I used to be more like Mom, loving art, painting, staring at a sunset for hours and doing nothing. But when she left—" *Left* seemed so much softer than *died*.

"He's built a bridge to you, Cami. Through the business. He's loving you in his own way."

"Is he?" Her eyes were beacons in the darkness when she looked at him. "I appreciate your insight. I know I should be grateful. But I still miss my mom. A lot."

"My parents are alive, and I miss them. I get busy and forget to call. Months go by. When I do call, it's hard to hear because their cell service is spotty."

"Do yourself a favor when you're in Sydney. Call them."

"I will." Something in her admonition stirred him. He had a choice to make. "You know, Dad left the inn to be a missionary. He always told me, 'Do what you're called to do.'"

"I'm moving to Indianapolis because my dad, my boss, told me to go. Am I called?" Cami's voice was low, tender. "Who knows? By the way, who does this mysterious calling? The universe? Fate? Life? Our own inner voice? God, if He actually cares?"

"Ah, she'll take Life's Hard Questions for a thousand, Alex."

Cami laughed. "I guess it is sort of late to be so philosophical."

And then he knew. If he was going to sell the inn, it needed to remain. To be a vital part of Hearts Bend business. He needed, wanted it to be loved. Cami loved it, like he did. The decision was clear. Easy to make.

"I'll take your offer, Cami."

She was silent a beat. She stopped and looked up at him. "The offer for the inn? You'll sell to me?"

"Yes."

She started to hug him, then stepped back and stuck out her hand. "Gentlemen's agreement."

He laughed and shook her hand. "A woman's agreement." He resisted the urge to tug her to him, wrap her in his arms and kiss her until—

"Ben, I promise I'll take care of it."

He nodded, emotion stealing his words. He'd just sold his grandparents' lifework. But this was the right choice. He was sure of it.

"Will you take care of the staff, Cami?" he said. "Myrtle May lives in the owner's cottage, but I'll give her part of the sale for a house. But she'll want to work. I think she'd be lost without it. Walt lives in his grandfather's fishing shack. He says, 'It's warm and dry, enough for this old bachelor.' Ray lives down the road. Has his own garden and fishing pond he keeps up too."

"I'll look out for them, Ben." Cami found his hand in the dark and linked her fingers with his. "And thank you for today, for selling me the inn."

"You're welcome. I trust you, Cami. I do." Hands still linked, he walked her around to the passenger side door. Moonlight drifted through the trees, and he could think of nothing, feel nothing, but her nearness.

He opened the door, but when she didn't slip into the seat, he gripped her waist and drew her close.

Cami's breath brushed against his cheek as if she might speak, but when she didn't, Ben tilted toward her and swept the curls that had fallen from her ponytail from her neck. She trembled with a low, nervous laugh, broke her hand from his and cradled her cheek against his neck, then cooled his hot skin with a soft, tender kiss.

Ben moved to see her face, to see the light in her eyes before he slowly touched his lips to hers.

She raised her face to his and, forgetting all hesitation, he kissed her again, soft and slow at first, then with a passionate pulse.

Ben walked Cami the step backward until she was pressed against the side of the truck, holding onto him and rising to meet his kiss. Breathing in, breathing out—

Around them, the wind stirred up a cricket chorus for a romantic serenade and rattled the leaves in harmonic rhythm.

Ben's hand slipped toward her hip, and that's when it

happened. A firework shot off just outside the parking lot, and their beautiful, incredible kiss ended with a laugh. Behind them, a group of teenage boys set off another firework, the noise echoing among the cars.

"My, my," Cami said, patting her forehead, then her hair. "You've improved, Ben Carter. That was *way* better than our first kiss."

"Same to you, Cami Jackson." He paused to clear the roughness from his voice. "Though it's disappointing we ended again with another *crack*, this time a firecracker—"

"But I loved the laugh."

"Kissing and laughing." He kissed her forehead. "What could be better?" Ben moved aside for Cami to climb in the passenger seat. "Guess we should go."

Cami started for the cab, then turned back to him. "Today was one for my diary, Ben, if I kept one."

He stepped closer, tucking her against his chest. "Yes, but I wish..."

"Ben, I can't move to Sydney. You can't move to Indianapolis." She hugged him with her cheek against his chest. "Are we to always be out of step with each other?"

"Seems like it." He ran his fingers down her back and back up. "What if we put your mom's painting on the ground and jump into it? Be the couple on the bench."

She pressed her hand to his cheek. "That would be lovely, but we live in the real world, Ben. You know we can't fall in love. Besides, the bench is gone."

Ben tapped his forehead to hers. "We'll find a new bench." Just like that, he was pretty sure he was falling in love with her.

"We should go," she said.

Ben held the door as she climbed in. He drove slowly back to the inn, wanting to linger in Cami's presence, which had him rethinking everything he believed about himself, his life, and his future.

Back at work, and she was still smiling from the Fourth weekend. From the last three weekends, really. She'd danced with Ben. Won a three-legged race with Ben. Acquired the inn. Kissed Ben. *Sigh.* Cami still buzzed at the memory of his lips.

She felt like a different woman when she was with him. She felt like herself.

Then Sunday had come with real world realities. More showings of her condo and helping Annalise with Vicki's wedding. The country star had finally agreed on a theme, colors, and menu. Annalise said it felt like a *rock* star accomplishment. But to Cami, she still looked tired, not her usually bubbly self.

The move to Indy was becoming more and more real. Astrid had texted Monday before 7:00 a.m. that Ben's contract was ready to sign. Once he signed the offer, the Akron paperwork would happen almost automatically.

When Cami arrived in the office a little before eight, she emailed the contract to Ben with a soft personal touch. "I had fun this past weekend."

He emailed back right away. "Give me a few days to go over this. Ben. P.S. I had a great time with you."

She smiled. All over. Right down to her Louis Vuitton–clad toes.

But she had Akron work to do. The inn could wait. Top of her list was to invite Astrid to join her in Indy. Cami wasn't sure she could do the job without her.

"Sorry I'm late." Astrid came in with her iPad and a mocha and took the seat across from Cami. She said that every week.

"You're not late." Cami's reply every week.

Astrid smirked, her blonde hair, pinned up on the sides, swaying as she shook her head. "How was your weekend? Did you see Ben? You must've, because you're smiling." Astrid made a face, peeking over the lid of her mocha.

"I always smile."

"Not like that." Astrid pointed to Cami as she set her coffee down. "Did you go over the résumés I sent you?"

"No." Cami leaned back in her chair, unable to stifle her smile, feeling for a flash moment like she was fifteen again. "I'll do it today. How was your weekend?"

"My weekend? You see I'm not smiling." The sadness in Astrid's voice was palpable.

"Sounds like things aren't improving with you and Boyfriend."

"He says he loves me, but—" Her eyes filled, and a small tear tipped the corner of her eye. She caught it with the edge of her finger as she focused on her iPad. "Let's get to work. We have a lot to do this week."

Cami walked around her desk and perched on the edge in front of Astrid. "This may not be the right time to ask, but will you come to Indy with me? I need you. I'm not sure—"

"Oh, Cami." Astrid launched to her feet and wrapped Cami in a tight hug. "I thought you'd never ask."

Cami laughed and breathed in Astrid's spicy perfume. "You could've asked."

The woman stepped back, wiping her eyes. "I know this will sound so stupid, but I've been waiting five years for Boyfriend to propose. Face it, he's not going to, is he? I would've asked you for the job, but I don't know, I guess I needed someone to ask me. To make me feel loved, needed, and..." Astrid covered her sob with her hand. "Feel special. I'm sorry I'm blubbering. It's so unprofessional."

"No, it's not. You're human. You have a right to weep over things that break or hurt your heart. Even in the workplace." Cami tugged a tissue from the box on her credenza. "Now, let's go over our schedule so you can get back to your desk and start looking for a place to live. Akron will pay for your relocation costs. And I'll have your new salary to you by the end of the day."

"Really? I'm at the top of my salary range. Brant will—"

"Sign it. I'll stand over him until he clicks all the approval boxes and sends the copy to human resources." She would, too, because Astrid deserved a raise.

"Cami, you're the best boss ever."

As they worked, they nailed down details for the week, booked a trip up to Indy.

"Let's do as much as we can from here. I'd rather not go up to Indy until next month." Cami opened up the résumés they'd collected.

"Brant's not going to like that."

"He doesn't have a choice." Cami shrugged as she scanned another résumé.

"You know, if Geoffrey was willing to relocate, he'd be an excellent project manager." Astrid tucked some hair behind her ear.

"Geoffrey is Brant's man." Dad had hired him and groomed him. Geoffrey was good—not as good as her, thank you very much—but Geoffrey was loyal to Dad and would be a spy, monitoring her every move. A not-so-secret spy.

Astrid nodded. "I'm not sure you'll have a choice. I think Geoffrey is angling for a move."

"He's qualified to lead as director. I can't imagine he'd be okay coming to work for me as second-in-command." There was no way she'd take a man who would report her every move back to Dad.

At ten, they had a call with the contractor. Dad had already approved the layout before he'd told Cami about the transfer. The building had been gutted, new windows put in, and the walls re-drywalled. He'd even repaired some electrical wires. At eleven, Cami had a Zoom tour with Max. She passed on the apartment, but Astrid had chatted the Realtor up, giving him much more to work with than Cami's non-enthusiastic specifications.

They'd just ordered lunch when Brant entered Cami's office. His presence filled the room. "Got a sec?"

His nod of dismissal had Astrid scurrying to the door. She mouthed *good luck* and shut the door behind her.

Cami stood. "Sure, we just ordered lunch."

"Then I won't take much time." There was a spark in his eyes above his calm demeanor. "Jeremy was reviewing your project schedule and saw you added the Hearts Bend Inn."

"Yes, I bought it Fourth of July weekend."

"You didn't tell me."

"I don't tell you about every acquisition."

"But this is the inn," Dad said, his tone conveying what his words did not.

"All the more reason not to involve you. Ben Carter inherited the place from his grandparents, but he works for Viridian Jewel Resorts and is opening a new place in Sydney. I sent him the contract this morning. I'll close with him the fifteenth of August."

"Cami, I don't want the inn. Withdraw the contract." No give. No take. Just a command. It was like she was twelve years old, not a twenty-nine-year-old professional. "There's no ROI."

"There will be. If you saw the project board, you saw my initial projections. We'll have to invest some money but, Dad, Hearts Bend Inn is a landmark. It's in a prime location. All we need is some investment capital. I'll run everything with Astrid from Indy, don't worry."

"Drop the project, Cami."

She stepped around her desk to face him, but she couldn't meet his gaze. "Just like that? Drop it? I gave my word, and isn't our word golden around here? One of our values? At the very least, let's renovate and sell it. We could get one point eight to two million for it. How is that not a good ROI?"

"Camellia, as your boss, I'm telling you to stop. We are property developers, not property *managers*." Dad turned for the door, paused, and with his head down, hands in his pockets, added, "As your father, I'm asking. Do *not* buy the inn." His voice was so low she could barely hear him. "Please."

Cami dropped into a chair. Dad's simple, vulnerable *please* struck her heart and sank deep.

"You're serious."

"Yes."

"Then I'll withdraw the offer. But it's going to cost us our earnest money."

"Fine. It's a write-off."

When Dad left, Cami felt winded and stunned. She couldn't move she was shaking so much. What had just happened? Emotion from her dad? There was so much more to his story. Would he ever share it with her?

CHAPTER 9

*H*ow was Cami going to tell Ben? She wasn't going to buy the inn. After convincing him to sell it to her. She parked next to his truck and glanced up at the restaurant—Angelo's. It was becoming a thing.

She'd waited a day to see if Dad would change his mind, but when he hadn't, she'd called Ben and asked to meet for dinner.

She'd tossed and turned all night. What was behind Dad's soft, emotional, humble *please?* It had nothing to do with the inn's ROI. Cami guessed it had everything to do with Mama.

The turmoil had also diminished her memories of Ben. She couldn't remember the taste of his kiss. After she gave him the news, he'd probably never kiss her again.

Did she want the inn? Yes. But Dad had stood in her office and *asked* her to let this deal go. *Please.*

She heard, even felt, the tenor of his voice every time she thought of it. *Since* she could count on one hand the number of times Dad had *asked* her for something, she would rescind the offer without further delay. Ben would just have to understand.

Cami glanced down at her Jimmy Choos, straightened her pencil skirt, and touched her hair. Smile in place, she headed inside Angelo's.

The cool, dim restaurant had a date-night feel. The string quartet played in the corner, and two couples danced on the open floor. The comforting scents of fresh Italian food filled the air.

Ben waved to her from the back booth—their booth. He stood and smiled as she approached, brushing his lips against her cheek. Her skin warmed under his touch, and she lingered to inhale his clean, soapy scent.

"You look beautiful." Ben gestured toward the table. "Professional."

"Came from work."

"You sounded like you had something on your mind when you called."

"Yeah, I do." The server arrived with a glass of sweet tea for Cami.

"I hope you don't mind, but I ordered a large pepperoni pizza, extra pepperoni, for us and sweet teas. But we can knock the work stuff out and then just be us."

Just be us. There might not be any "us" after she told him she couldn't buy the inn. Would he think she'd been toying with him?

Ben reached for a folder sitting next to him on the bench and slid it across the table. His eyebrows lifted as he smirked. "I didn't need *forty-eight hours* to sign the contract. Signed them the moment you sent them."

"You'll never let me live that down, will you?"

"A woman who can imitate *The Godfather?* No, I don't think I will."

Cami reached for the folder and opened it to see Ben's signature scrolled on the bottom of the paper.

"I am glad you'll be the one to take the inn. It was a hard decision to sell, but when you told me your vision of a retreat for artists and families, I knew you would carry on my grandparents' tradition. Makes the decision bearable." Ben reached across the table for Cami's hand. "I'm glad you're the one behind the deal."

His blue eyes held her captive. The feeling his kiss had left on her cheek faded. She pulled her hand back. "That's just it, Ben. I can—"

"One large extra-pepperoni pizza." The server set a steaming pizza on the table, forcing Ben and Cami to lean back. The scents of melted cheese, spicy pepperoni, and garlic filled the air.

"Good timing. We were just finished with our business for the night. Now we celebrate and relax."

"I'll be back with more sweet tea," the waiter said. "*Bon appétit.*"

Ben plated a slice of pizza for her, then one for himself. Steam lifted off the melting cheese, and the delicious aroma made her stomach growl. She'd been too stressed about this dinner to eat lunch.

"So, what else is new?" Ben said, taking a big bite of his slice. "How's Indy going? If you have time this weekend, I can show you around the inn with the eye of the owner instead of as a potential buyer."

Tell him.

"Can you come up Thursday evening?" When he looked at her, the candlelight danced in his eyes. "The drive-in is showing *Grease.*"

"Um, *Grease?* Sure." *Stop stalling. Tell him.*

But being with Ben was so easy. They talked about the upcoming college football season, the Titans, the latest Hearts Bend news. But the impending conversation hung over her head and distracted her.

When the waiter cleared away the pizza, Ben led Cami to the dance floor. She slid her hand into his—the hand of a man who did funny things to her heart.

He held her close and moved her in a slow, easy sway, his chest a wall under her hand. His cheek rested against hers, and he hummed along with the quartet.

Just be, Cami. She closed her eyes, shutting out any protest, any fear, any worry of what was to come, and enjoyed this dance, this moment, this man.

"Cami," he said, "I hate to bring us back to reality, but now that I've sold the inn, I'm leaving for Sydney Friday. I'll be gone two weeks. I'll come back to sign the final papers. Then it's Down Under for good."

"We knew this moment was coming."

"Doesn't make it easier." He peered into her eyes. "You started to say something just as the pizza arrived. What was it?"

"Did I?" He looked so happy, so content. He was about to embark on a long journey with a heavy-duty job ahead of him. Why not keep the news until he got back? It wouldn't change much in the long run. Besides, she loved this moment, being in his arms, turning to the music. Yes, the news could wait. "I can't remember. Must not have been important."

She placed her head on his chest. The steady beat of his heart was in tune with hers. Ben rested his cheek on her head. In his arms, she felt like she'd found a piece of herself she hadn't known was missing.

"Cami," he said, "I might want this to last."

Leaning back slightly, she searched his eyes and pressed her hand against his cheek.

His lips brushed hers, and she swooned at his gentle caress.

"How can this last, Ben?" Was there a possibility of a

future for them? Did they have a love that could last? "Our paths are literally on different hemispheres."

"You and your realities." Ben kissed the top of her head. "No more talk about work or about different paths. Let's just enjoy tonight."

"Agreed." See, she couldn't tell him. They'd just agreed not to talk about work, and she was a woman of her word.

"I need your signature." Jordan handed Ben an iPad as he crossed the marble and steel lobby toward the manager's office. Ben had been in Sydney one week, and he'd fallen into an easy routine. He missed the unpredictability of the schedule he'd kept in Hearts Bend, and the time difference made talking with Cami tricky.

The engineers had just connected the lobby fountain, and the crew was now serenaded by bubbling water. Light flooded the space from the domed ceiling, and the Emerald had a "lost in paradise" tropical feel.

It had been Ben's idea to give the Emerald's front entrance a lush, tropical garden ambiance, and so far, they were on track for a world-class lobby.

"What am I signing?" Ben said as he scribbled his name. "Please tell me this is for the towels."

"And the tablecloths. The lads are unloading the crates now. We'll have them laundered by the end of the week."

Ben and Jordan headed in different directions at Ben's office. Sitting at his neat, orderly desk that had no pictures of the people he loved, he kicked off his leather shoes. He missed his sneakers and work boots at the inn.

He missed Hearts Bend, and keeping in touch with Cami was hard, seeing as they were in radically different time zones.

They kept up a running text conversation, but the reality of keeping a relationship going with Cami faded by the moment.

Ben grabbed a bottle of Mount Franklin water and returned to his desk. Taking a long swig, he reviewed the checklist on his screen.

Lobby paintings were hung and the wall texture complete. The commissioned sculpture by a local artist was due at the end of the week. The lighting was installed, and tonight they would test the light board for effects.

A group from Hong Kong had toured the Emerald this morning and signed a contract to begin the Jade Resort and Spa in the next two years. There was a dinner to celebrate in a half hour.

Jim had been impressed with the Hong Kong success. He'd clapped Ben on the shoulder after they left.

I wasn't sure you were keeping on top of things while in that Podunk town, but you've proved me wrong. Well done.

Ben had turned the praise around on Jordan. He couldn't have done any of this without him.

Another pass over the checklist, and Ben swirled his chair to look out over the harbor. The Opera House reflected on the water as a sailboat floated by. He'd been dreaming of this view since he'd gotten the assignment, but now that he was here, he missed the quiet garden and green fields outside the inn's office window.

And this fancy, expensive office chair was not near as comfortable as Granddaddy's old leather squeaker. Maybe he'd have the chair shipped over. And pack the picture of Granny and Granddaddy that sat on the desk.

Cami wouldn't mind. Though, she'd hire a manager who would probably bring in an ergonomic chair or even a yoga ball.

He slid open the window and breathed in the saline air of the harbor. But oh, he missed the fresh Tennessee air, the scent of the grass after a rainstorm. He even missed Myrtle May's off-key singing, and Bart trailing after her.

But what he missed more than anything? The feel of Cami in his arms and her sweet sigh after he kissed her.

But he had no time to dream of a woman thousands of miles away. He had just enough time for a quick nap before dinner. A week in Sydney and he was still jet-lagged.

He moved to the office couch and stretched out. He'd just started to drift off when his phone buzzed. He grinned. Another text from Myrtle May.

Walt made tuna again. Whole place smells like onions. It's gross. But the Collinses checked in and raved about the scent of lunch. I think they're aliens.

He hoped she continued these texts after the sale. She was the sports commentator of the inn's happenings.

Ray said he replaced some coils or something in the AC unit of Cottage Two. Do I need to be texting all this to Cami Jackson?

He'd left a list for Ray. Myrtle May's play-by-plays let him know Ray was ticking through the list faster than Ben ever had. The man had more energy in his seventies than Ben at thirty.

He set his phone on the coffee table and tried to drift off again, but thoughts of Hearts Bend kept him awake. Here he was, in his dream city working his dream job, and he missed, even ached for, that old-fashioned inn and his zany aunt and grumpy cook.

He missed Cami, and the thought of not seeing her this weekend bugged him. He sat up. Where was this thought process going? He refused to abandon his life plan and goals for the passing affection of a beautiful woman. But was it passing?

Besides, he'd already signed the inn over to her. When he went back to Hearts Bend, he'd sign the final papers and be done.

She'd warned against falling in love, and look, that's exactly what he'd done. Ben jumped up from the sofa. He was in love with Cami Jackson.

He grabbed his phone and started a text but then glanced at his watch. Half an hour until dinner, which didn't leave enough time to text Cami an "I love you" message. Did he even want to text her something so personal and intimate?

On impulse, he called his father. He needed to talk to someone now.

"Ben, hello. This is a surprise."

"Hey, Dad. I'm in Sydney, so I thought I'd say hi while we're in the same time zone." He returned to his chair and turned toward the view.

"You're in Sydney already? I thought you were hanging out in Hearts Bend until September."

"I needed to make a trip down to oversee some things, but I'm heading home in a few days." *Home.* The word slipped from his lips easily. "Dad, I'm selling the inn to Cami Jackson, who I think I might be in love with."

His dad's whistle came through the phone. "That's a lot in one sentence."

"We have twenty-four minutes to solve my life problems." He laughed. "I'm due at a dinner with the Hong Kong team."

"Let's start with the inn. You sold it?"

Ben listed all the issues, the bank loan, and his desire to keep his career on track. "If I didn't sell, I'd have to deal with the debt and renovations."

"Mom was never good with money, but whenever I asked if she needed help, she said she was fine. Said Stan at the bank was looking after her."

"She said the same thing to me. She didn't want us to worry."

"Who did you sell to again? Cami Jackson, the little girl with dark curls? You always liked her."

"That's the one."

"I remember her. Cute kid. Granny didn't care for her dad too much. Brant. Said he would level Hearts Bend if he had his way."

"She exaggerated, but yeah, he is pretty hard core. Cami works for him, but the inn is sort of her private project. Dad, she's beautiful. I think I love her."

Dad was quiet for a few beats. "I like hearing you're in love, but it doesn't sound simple."

Ben explained how her career was taking her to Indianapolis but she wanted the inn as a memorial to her mother. "She died in Cottage Three."

"I remember. Mom was really upset."

"She started coming down to the inn and, well—"

"You tripped and fell in love."

"Dad, what do I do? I can't walk away from Viridian without huge consequences. I have no idea if she feels the same about me. She's pretty ensconced in the family business."

"I know you're going to think this is a cliché answer but, Ben, if you want guidance, you should ask the One who made you."

Ben smiled at Dad's answer. Should've known that's what he'd say. Ben found it comforting. "Mr. Graham said that too."

"Larry Graham? He always did offer good advice."

So did Dad. But would God really hear him? Was He really interested in his prayers? The Sunday school answer was yes. Ben knew that Dad believed it. But since the day they'd left him in Hearts Bend, Ben hadn't been so sure God was listening.

"I'm not sure I'd know if He answered."

Dad took his time responding. "Ben, talking to God, believing He hears us, simply requires faith. It's something we need in our daily life. Real faith kicks in when the going gets tough. When we can't see what's next. Real faith is trusting in God when we can't see a way through. So maybe right now, when you don't know which way to go and you're looking for direction, exercise a bit of faith and to talk to Him."

As a missionary, Dad lived and breathed his faith. Ben didn't have that claim. "God didn't hear me when I asked for my parents to come back for me."

He'd not planned to bring *that* up. But the words were out now.

"Son." Dad's voice deepened. "Leaving you in Hearts Bend was the hardest thing your mom and I have ever done. But I had to protect you. When you were six, the typhoon threat scared me, but then after you wandered off and went missing for a night, fear gripped our lives. I couldn't stop thinking about the what-ifs. What if we hadn't found you? What if someone else found you? What if you'd fallen? What if you were hurt? I was sure I'd never find you. But the Lord came through and made it clear your future was in Hearts Bend."

"You've never told me any of this. You said you'd come back for me in the summer, but you didn't."

"We couldn't leave. We both had malaria, remember?"

"Yeah, I think so." He'd been six at the time, and the adults hadn't shared a lot of details. Only that staying in Hearts Bend was the best for him.

"Turns out you have a knack for the hotel business and a gift to work with people. Look how your career has taken off. Being in Hearts Bend was God prepping you for your future."

God had prepared him? When? During the afternoons with Granddaddy fixing the plumbing or rebuilding the gazebo? When Granny showed him how to make a bed and clean the stove? Maybe it was the Saturday mornings with Ray in the garden.

How did Cami fit into God's planning? Everything pointed to the inn, so why was he sitting in Sydney?

A knock sounded on his door, and Ben looked up to see Jordan pointing at his watch. "Dad, just a sec. Jordan, I'll be there in a few minutes. Tell them to get started without me." He pointed to the phone. "Emergency."

After telling Ben to talk to God, there wasn't much more for Dad to say. He offered to pray for Ben as they ended the conversation, and to his surprise, Ben said, "That'd be nice."

Making his way to the Emerald's lavish dining hall, Ben whispered his own prayer. "Don't know if I have enough faith for this, God, but if You have any ideas on why I suddenly want to be in Hearts Bend instead of Sydney, I'd appreciate the insight. Thanks and, well, amen."

"$\mathcal{M}$arta has three offers on my condo. All above asking." Cami poured hot water over an English Breakfast tea bag on a calm Saturday morning and placed the stainless-steel kettle back on the electric stovetop in her sister's kitchen.

"Already? Good for you. So you're not going to lease it?" Annalise sat at her kitchen table, the sun streaming in through the windows, lighting the whitewashed table.

"Marta doesn't think there's a market for leasing. And she's got three good offers. She is a Realtor, after all. When I come back, I'll find an even better place. The loft was almost too small for me anyway. Are you sure you want hot tea? It's a thousand degrees outside. I can ice it for you."

"I'll take it hot. With a little cream and honey, like Mama used to make it."

Cami went through the motions of making the tea, just like Mama always had when they weren't feeling well. Not that Annalise would ever admit to feeling less than a hundred percent.

"How was Indy?"

"Busy." Cami sank into the chair across from her sister. "The office space Dad bought is going to be really classy when the build-out is done."

"What about the apartment listings? Did any of those work out for you?"

Cami shook her head. "None of them felt like home." In fact, the only place that felt like home these days was the inn. Which she would never own.

"You're running out of time. You need to find a place. It doesn't have to be permanent. Just until you do find the place that you can call home."

"That's just it. I'm not sure I want to call Indy home."

"Is this about the inn?"

"Maybe. And Ben. I don't know. You should've seen Dad, Annalise. Standing in my office, head down, hands in his pockets, saying please."

"He doesn't feel about the inn like you do."

"I wish he'd talk to me."

"Why don't you talk to him?"

"I might." Cami leaned toward her sister. "Did you see a doctor? You're looking brighter."

"I told you it was food poisoning from sushi."

"For a month?"

"It's not been a month."

"Almost."

Annalise raised her eyebrow, giving Cami that look, the one that said she wouldn't say anymore.

Fine. She'd let it go. For now. "How's things with the great wedding?"

"Going well. She's calmed down a bit." Annalise sipped her tea with a bit of a smile on her lips. "What's going on with you? I can tell something is bothering you."

"Did you hear me say Dad said 'Please'?"

"Don't sound so shocked. He says please all the time."

"Not when it comes to an Akron deal. I'm telling you, he was contrite, soft-spoken... Not the usual bulldog Brant Jackson demanding his way.

"I don't think he's gotten over Mama's death. He holds it all in," Annalise said.

"He holds it against me."

Annalise peered at Cami over the edge of her cup. "I know you think he does, but you're wrong. You're his daughter. If you really believe he blames you, talk to him."

"And then have it confirmed that Mama's death was my responsibility? No thanks."

"How is death anyone's responsibility? God gives and takes life."

"Because I was there, Annalise." Cami scooted back from the table and stared out the sink window. The image of Mama lying on the cottage floor had only dulled slightly with time. "I didn't help her."

"You were fifteen and your mom collapsed, not breathing. What were you supposed to do?"

"I tried CPR, I—" She turned to her sister. "Sorry, I didn't mean to bring all this up. I've put it behind me, and it should stay behind me. I wanted to buy the inn as a memorial to Mama, but Dad clearly has issues with it."

"Have you ever considered that he blames himself? That he wasn't with her when she died. That he'd become a workaholic."

Cami considered her sister's insight. "I can't see Brant Jackson blaming himself."

"So, no inn? What about Ben?"

Ben, sweet Ben. Cami had tried to text him the truth a couple of times but couldn't bring herself to hit Send. She'd let him and herself down by not telling him that night at Angelo's. The last two weeks had also proved it would be impossible to have a long-distance relationship. Not that she was actually counting on an Australia-to-America romance.

Meeting up every Fourth would most likely not happen. Life would get in the way. But she had her memories of this summer.

"I met Ben for dinner to tell him I couldn't buy the inn, but he'd already signed the contract. He said he could go to Sydney in peace knowing the inn was in good hands."

"So you didn't tell him?"

"No, and I feel really horrible about it. I've lost sleep over it."

"That's not fair, Cami. He's been gone two weeks thinking the inn was taken care of. What's he going to do when he comes home? Scramble to find a solution?"

"I know, I know." She peered in her teacup as if to find an answer. "I've decided to call in every favor I have to get him a new buyer. One who will care about the place."

"You could always just tell Dad you want it. I know you long for his approval, but you're twenty-nine, Cami. You're a savvy businesswoman who can make her own decisions."

"Annalise, I tell you, if you'd seen him…" Cami sipped her tea. "There's more to the story. Astrid found the contract on my desk and put it in the system as a pending sale, which means inspections and surveys are automatically being scheduled."

"Oh, Cami. You didn't tell her?"

"Didn't think I needed to tell her. Dad will be furious. He won't be the contrite man saying, 'Please.' But I still have to tell Ben I can't buy it. And that really pains me. I like him. I want his respect too. And I hate breaking contracts."

"Dad won't be furious, and if he is, so what? Maybe you'll have the discussion you've needed to have for years." Annalise reached across the table for Cami's hand. "My dear sister, Ben will understand. As for Dad, he'll get over himself. But you, stop blaming yourself for Mama's death. You walk around like you have to be perfect and make up for something you didn't do."

"I do not think I have to be perfect."

"Yes, you do. For Dad, now Ben. Cami, listen to me. I'll say it again. God is the giver and taker of life. You have to trust Him that He loved Mama more than any of us, and if that summer day had not been her time, she'd still be here. Sweetie, she had a heart attack and was dead before she hit the ground."

"I remember. She clutched her chest, cried out, and fell to the ground."

"Then you *know* it's not your fault."

"You know what Dad said to me. 'When it's my time, I hope your sister is there. She'll know what to do. She'll not *let* me die.'"

"He didn't mean it. He was angry. Hurt. Scared. Had lost the love of his life. Now he had to raise two daughters alone. He lashed out. It wasn't right, but don't let his words hang over you like a fog."

"Me? He's the one in the fog. I will always be the girl who let her mom die."

"Then maybe it's time for you to make a stand. Step away. Find what you're looking for. Find peace and forgiveness. There is Someone who wants you to find Him. Someone waiting for you to call out to Him."

Cami smiled and dabbed her eyes with the edge of her napkin. "Mama always brought everything back to her faith. When did you start?"

"I never stopped. I just didn't push it on you. Cami, God doesn't blame you. It was Mama's time. She is happier, healthier, and better off in heaven. She's singing praises, painting extraordinary pictures."

"You're right. And I guess she'd tell me to let go of the past. Including the inn. It would be a lot to oversee renovations from Indianapolis. I'd have to hire a manager to run things." Deciding she was hungry, Cami grabbed some cheddar cheese and an apple out of the fridge. "I did see it, though, as a haven for people like Mama. Artists, or anyone really, who need an escape or a refuge."

"But it's in the system, right? Are you going ahead with it? Dad can just deal."

"I'm not sure I'm brave enough to face him. I can deal with hard-nosed buyers without batting an eye, but Dad is a different beast."

"Does Ben Carter have anything to do with your desire to buy the inn?"

Excitement shot through her at the mention of Ben's name. "It's not about Ben, but I really don't want to let him down." Cami cut up the cheese and apples, plated them with some crackers, and placed them in the center of the table. "Do you remember how much time we spent in the pool at the inn? We used to beg Dad to build us one in our backyard."

Annalise reached for an apple slice. "He never did. Secretly, I think he liked going to spend time by the pool as much as we did. But he eventually stopped going."

"See? Good memories. I just feel like if someone else buys the inn, they're going to change it too much or knock it down. If it was any other property, that's what I'd do. But if that happens, we'll lose the last real memory of Mama as well as Ben's grandparents."

"We have all kinds of memories of Mama. Ben has the ones with his grandparents. But some of my favorite family memories are the church picnics or family game nights. How Mama really went all out for our birthdays and the holidays."

Cami grabbed a slice of apple and topped it with a bite of cheese. "I gave up church, and Dad sold the house. Maybe I don't want to give up all things related to Mama."

"Then find your faith. Of all the things you're doing, Mama would want you to have faith. Determine to trust God with your career, with Dad, even with Ben. It can't be like that half-marathon we used to dream of running but never trained for. You have to make time to get to know the One you need to trust."

She was right, which irritated Cami just a touch. Mama had brought them up in church, taught them to pray, to love God. But talking to Him after Mama died had seemed futile. He never answered her question, *Why did You let it happen?* If she couldn't trust Him to keep Mama safe, how could she trust Him with anything else?

"Maybe I need to get back to God, but how does that help me now with the inn debacle?"

"Talk to God about it. See what He does." Annalise reached for another slice of apple and cheddar cheese. "Tell Dad it's too late; the sale of the inn is in the system."

"It's easy to be so bold when we're at your kitchen table."

She tried to picture walking into Dad's office with a bold *I'm buying the inn.* She felt herself shrink back at the very idea.

But picturing telling Ben she couldn't buy the inn after all made her shrink all the more.

God, a little help?

If she let Ben down, he'd be gone in a few weeks, back to Australia for good. She'd be in Indianapolis and wouldn't have to see him again. Which was a sad yet oddly comforting thought.

But Dad? She'd have to deal with him daily. And for all her

success and achievements, the fifteen-year-old Cami still yearned for her father to hold her and tell her everything was going to be all right.

One more ping on his phone, and Ben would turn it off.

It had started when Jim called at five in the morning. He'd flown out a few days ago, and Ben wasn't even sure where he was or what time it was there, but it had been way too early in Sydney to receive a phone call from his fuming boss.

The door locks have been returned. Peter in accounting said we were just credited with a refund. What is going on?

Ben had stumbled out of bed and turned on the coffee, trying to follow Jim's demands. Last he had heard, the locks had been shipped and were on their way. He had no idea why they'd been returned and the company credited their payment.

Eight hours later, he still didn't have an answer. And he was shaking from drinking too much coffee. He'd been on hold with the locksmith company for an hour, and now the music played in his office while he read his texts from Myrtle May. They were the one bright spot in his day.

Walt and his tuna. It's not even Tuesday. When you get back will you convince him it's not Tuna Tuesday and I'd much rather have tacos?

Maybe just convince him that it's never a good day for tuna.

We have four new reservations for the end of the month.

Cami hasn't been by since you've been gone. Did you make her angry? Don't mess things up with her. I like her.

Jordan knocked on his office door, and Ben looked up, rubbed his hand down his face, and nodded toward a chair. His assistant shook his head. "Jim's on the other line. I'll listen to the hold music in my office so you can chat with the boss. Give me thirty seconds, then put this call on hold. I'll pick it up in my office, and you can talk with Jim. Line three."

Ben counted to thirty, took a deep breath, and put his line on hold. He watched the light change colors, indicating Jordan had picked up. Ben answered line three.

"Hello, Jim. Still trying to work things out with the locks. You'll be the first to know—"

"Ben, you'll figure out those locks. I'm calling with good news for you. The Hong Kong execs were so pleased with the Emerald, they want you to sign on with them when they break ground next year. That will give you time to get the Emerald up and running before you transfer. If the Jade is a success, you'll be eligible for a director position in the home office."

Home office. Wow. It's what he'd been hoping for, working toward. To hear it spoken as a possibility in the near future...

Ben closed his eyes and let his chin fall on his chest—after the early morning call, it was all he could muster in the way of excitement.

Was Dad right? Was this what God had been preparing him for? If so, why was his excitement minimal? This was what he'd been working for. His long-term goal, and he could only muster a mental woo-hoo. A quiet mental cheer at that. Nothing more. Shouldn't he be jumping for joy like Tom Cruise on a couch?

"But before any of that can happen, the Emerald has to open smoothly."

"I'm working to make sure everything will run smoothly before I get on the plane in the morning."

"You're returning to the States?"

"Yes. I need to go back for closing."

"Then hurry back. Say mid-August? The Emerald is shining because of you, Ben, and you're on track to make director."

"I appreciate that, Jim. I won't let you down. I'll be back just as soon as I can. In the meantime, I'll handle things remotely, and Jordan is here." Closing was set for August fifteenth, and he still had a lot of his grandparents' belongings to clean out and pack before then. Hopefully, he could be on the plane the day after.

Jim hung up, and Ben felt exhausted instead of exhilarated. This trip to Sydney was supposed to cement his future, but instead he felt weary, lonely, and out of touch.

Out of touch...with Cami. He'd fly halfway around the world just to see her. Forget the inn and any closing. Moving to the window, he watched traffic buzz by. Sydney was an amazing city, but he missed the quiet streets of Hearts Bend and the fragrances of a Tennessee breeze. He missed the feeling of peace. He missed his relaxing Saturdays with Cami.

He pulled his phone out, ignoring the texts from Myrtle May, and sent a text to Cami.

Heading to HB tomorrow. You around? See you on Saturday?

It was late for Cami. She'd be wrapping up her day, getting ready for bed. She might already be in bed. But maybe he'd catch her.

He was about to tuck his phone away when her reply pinged in.

Have a safe flight. I'll see you Saturday. Are you sure you won't be jet-lagged?

I'm sure. See you soon.

The three dots appeared as if she had more to say, but then they disappeared, and she didn't text again.

At his computer, he started looking for a solution to the lock problem. He'd just have to call the manufacturer tomorrow. Then he opened his calendar to get a feel for how much time he had left to get a mountain of work done. But what stood out to him the most was he only had two weeks left with Cami. And it wasn't enough time.

It didn't matter how many times they said they'd just enjoy the moment—he wanted the moments to last. Would he ever have more than a summer romance with her?

CHAPTER 11

*T*his was the day. The day everything would change.

Maybe. If Cami could really stand up to Dad, tell him that she was keeping this project.

Please.

For all her bravado, she couldn't shake that one simple word. The whispered plea cut straight to Cami's heart.

She wanted the inn. More than anything, but not at the expense of her dad.

Ben was a businessman. He would understand. Sometimes contracts fell through.

Cami attempted to remove the property from the system, but it was locked by the project manager, and he'd traveled to another site with Dad. Cami didn't want to text him to give her access, because then he'd say something to Dad and...snowball upon snowball.

So she'd just wait until he got back. In the meantime, she had to get on with the business of telling Ben the deal was off.

On this gorgeous albeit hot July Saturday, she pulled up to the Hearts Bend Inn and parked under a shade tree. The morning breeze nipped at her as she stepped out and waved to Ben, who stood out front waiting for her.

Were her eyes deceiving her or did he look more handsome than when he left?

"G'day, mate." He managed the Australian with a perfect accent.

"Howdy, stranger," she said in her very best Southern.

His warm embrace was like coming home. The fresh scent of soap, the warm squeeze of his strong arms. She took a moment to draw from his strength.

"Ben, can we talk in your office?" Because today was a business meeting, and having a desk between them would remind her of her mission.

"Sure." He peered at her with a quizzical expression. "What's going on?"

Cami inhaled to fight a wave of emotion. She blamed the inn's magical grounds and the memories of Mama.

"I'll tell you in your office."

Ben gripped her hand and led them into the cool inn. Soft music piped through a speaker by the desk. Myrtle May hummed along as she clicked something on the computer before she looked up, her faithful dog curled up in his bed behind her.

"Cami, darling, welcome back." Myrtle May stepped from the desk to embrace her. The tears built behind Cami's eyes. "Or should I say welcome home, boss lady? I want you to know I offered a ten percent off for a three-night stay this month and we booked right up. Both cottages are rented, and we had a request for another. We need to get Cottage Three up and running, but I'll let you two work that out."

They stepped into the office, and Ben shut the office door as Cami sat in the antique chair across from the desk. He relaxed in a large, very worn but comfy-looking chair.

"You look good."

She smiled. She'd worn her yellow blouse and white pencil skirt, as if the colors would brighten the news she came bearing. "So do you."

"Cami, what's going on?" He scooted his chair around to sit next to her.

Cami gave him a side glance and tried to smile. *Stop hemming and hawing, Jackson.*

She put on her seven years of experience as a buyer like armor and did her job. "I can't buy the inn."

He raised an eyebrow, and his lips thinned. "Come again?"

"Since you signed the contract in good faith, Akron will pay the earnest fee. I'm terribly sorry."

He sat back with an exhale, regarding her, reading her. His eyebrows drew together as he studied her. "Is this about your dad?"

"He asked me to let this go."

Ben stood and paced around the desk, then back to his chair. "I should have known." His shoulders drooped, and disappointment bled into his words. "You may have had good intentions, but your dad calls the shots. I assume I can put it on the market tomorrow."

She made a face. "Not yet. The property got loaded into our system, and it's been locked by the admin for processing. I promise as soon as he gets back in town Monday I'll have it cleared. So if you could wait a few days... Maybe until late next week."

"Cami, that eats into my time. How am I going to sell this place in less than a month?"

"I'm going to call in every favor I have to get you a good buyer, Ben. One who will love this place for the next generation."

"But no one will love it like you. Or me."

"Maybe not, but there are plenty of people who love towns and establishments like Hearts Bend and the inn. There's a couple in Georgia who restore old buildings and open up shops or bed and breakfasts. They'd love the inn."

"Thank you, but it's not the same, is it? When I come home, if I come home, strangers will be running the place. At least with you, I felt like the inn was still in the family." He propped against the edge of the desk. "It made me feel close to you. I feel like I keep losing the things I love, but yet, I was the one who hightailed it out of town and joined the VJR team."

"Annalise helped me to see maybe Mama wanted me to return to my faith more than an old building. No offense."

"None taken. My dad said something similar. Said I should seek God for my future."

"Mama used to say God wasn't a genie in a bottle, but we should still take everything to Him in prayer. But He didn't seem to hear my prayers, so I stopped asking for things. I never got my wish."

"Dad says faith is hoping in the unseen. Maybe we're trying too hard to see everything when we should just trust."

"Maybe."

Maybe she needed to have faith in something, *someone*, bigger than herself. Like acknowledging she needed to trust God?

Cami slid her hand into his. "Then we'll have faith. Faith that everything is going to work out. And I'm still here. I'm heading to Indy in a few weeks, but for now, I'm here."

"Sure would be nice to jump into your mom's painting about now." Ben's gaze captured hers. Searching. She hoped he could see all that she couldn't say. How sorry she was for this.

"Sure would."

"Are you hungry?" Ben squeezed her hand. "Angelo's?"

Yes, a thousand times yes. But going to Angelo's would only

tug on her heart, and she needed to let him, let Ben and the inn, go.

"Actually, I need to get back. I'll get to work on this. Let you know when you can list it as soon as I can."

"I'll walk you out."

Their footsteps echoed in unison as they crossed the lobby. Cami slowed as they passed Mama's painting.

"I suppose you'll want to take that with you," Ben said.

"I'll come back for it."

As she walked to the car, she tried to commit the moment to memory. The fresh scent of a Tennessee summer afternoon. The quiet coo of a dove. The strong hand wrapped around hers.

Ben opened her car door, and she turned to say she was sorry again, but the words stuck in her throat. This seemed very final. Cami looked up into Ben's blue eyes and let her hand rest on his cheek. His close-trimmed beard was soft against her palm. She would miss him. She'd miss their connection.

He bent to her and pressed his lips to hers. A soft, gentle, goodbye kind of kiss.

Twenty-four hours had passed. Jack Bauer might be able to save the world in twenty-four hours, but Ben couldn't seem to let go of the conversation with Cami.

When he'd pulled out the contract to give to her at Angelo's, she'd seemed so surprised. He'd read that night all wrong. Rather than her excitement over the deal, had she been trying to figure out a way to tell him she no longer wanted the inn?

No longer wanted the inn.

Why hadn't she told him if she'd known? He'd lost two precious weeks. He could have had a new buyer by now. Cami had been in a tough spot. Did it change how he felt about her? She'd been honest with him, and it wasn't an easy conversation. He respected that. But the kiss before she left had felt like goodbye, and it had hurt to watch her drive away.

Sunday afternoon she'd texted the name of the couple in Georgia.

They are interested. Will check out the inn.

But could he sign over the inn to just any ole body? This put a whole new light on things. As much as he wanted the promotion Jim dangled in front of him, he wanted this inn to be in good hands. And those hands were his or Cami's.

Standing in the middle of the lobby, Ben inhaled the familiar and welcoming scent of Walt's snickerdoodle cookies. Soft piano music piped through the speakers. Two couples sat around a table in the dining area, drinking Walt's coffee and enjoying the cookies. They'd checked in earlier, regaling him with stories of their past stays in the inn.

"Ben?" He turned to see Iris, the housekeeper. "The toilet in Room Eight won't stop running. Can you please look at it? I'd call Ray but he's off on Sundays. Also, the doorknob is loose, and the painting on the wall was down. It needs to be rehung."

"Thanks, Iris. I'll have to run to the barn to get some supplies. Can you sit at the desk until Myrtle May returns?"

The warm sun burned against his skin, the humidity thick, as he hurried to the barn. If he was going to keep this place, he'd make sure there were some tools in the inn so he didn't have to trek out to the barn every time something was needed. He pulled at his collar as sweat dripped down his back. Especially in this heat.

Flowers swayed in the garden as the breeze whispered over the grounds. Overhead, thin wispy clouds drifted across the blue sky. Peaceful, tranquil, beautiful Hearts Bend, Tennessee, was vastly different than the hustle and bustle of Sydney.

Ben was almost to the barn when he heard a loud sneeze.

"Ray?" Ben followed another sneeze and found the gardener on his knees on a garden kneeling pad. His hands were covered in dirt with a trowel in hand, freshly planted lilies in a row in front of him.

"Iris said you were off today. What are you doing?"

"The preacher spoke on how the lilies neither toil nor spin but they are more regal than all of King Solomon's garb. Made me think I needed to trust the Lord more with my life."

"I'm right there with you, Ray." Ben bent to examine the lilies. They were beautiful. And God took complete care of them with the sun, rain, and soil.

Wasn't he at least as good as a lily?

"What brings you out to the barn today?"

"I needed a few things for Room Eight."

"Ah, is the toilet acting up again? I think you'll need to replace the flapper this time. I picked up a few from the hardware store last time I was there." Ray clapped his hand on Ben's shoulder. Little specks of dirt flew off and landed on the front of Ben's shirt. He wiped it clean. "What's on your mind? I can tell it's more than toilets."

"I was thinking of the lilies and how they don't have to worry about anything."

"Neither do you, Ben. Neither do you."

"Easier said than done."

"Want to tell ole Ray what's going on?"

"Lots of things. Cami told me she isn't buying the inn after all. So we're back to ground zero. When I walked her out, we stopped in front of her mother's painting. Ray, do you know what happened to the bench that used to be in the garden?"

"Can't say offhand that I do. Why?"

"I was just thinking it'd be nice to give to Cami along with the painting. Whoever buys the inn won't have any emotional attachment to it or the painting."

But he still had an emotional attachment to the inn and Cami. Following his heart would cost him his career. His future.

"I'll keep a lookout for it." Ray walked with Ben to the barn. Inside, Ray made his way to the box fan in the corner and turned it on, the air flow a welcome relief.

"I take it you're still heading to Sydney," Ray said.

"Sooner rather than later." Ben started walking between the shelves. "I'm getting a promotion out of this project if everything goes well."

"And the inn?"

"Cami actually might have a buyer. Not anyone connected to the inn, which would've been nice, but they won't knock it down."

"That's a heap of tomorrow's worries, ain't it? The fate of the inn, your job."

"Life comes with worry, Ray. To get ahead, you have to work hard, do things you don't often want to do, but in the end, your effort, your choice plays out."

"Even so, you still got to trust the One who clothed the lilies."

There it was. The Sunday school lesson. *Talk to God. Trust God.*

Ray wandered toward the wooden workbench and returned with a new flapper.

"Just like I knew we'd need this flapper, God knows your needs. He knows your tomorrows. Talk to Him, Ben. Let Him have your tomorrows."

Sure, okay, but it was way easier said than done.

CHAPTER 12

$\mathcal{C}$ami's Dior slingbacks clicked against the wooden floor on the top story of the Akron Development building, echoing along the quiet hall of the executive offices on Thursday morning. The normally active and busy office was quiet. Did the entire office know she was going to confront the boss and had hightailed it somewhere safe?

She wore her eggplant-colored power suit and had slicked back her hair into a businesslike chignon. Her makeup was bright but not overdone. Pink lips, not red.

After telling Ben she couldn't buy the inn, after carrying her father's gentle *please* around in her heart for two weeks, she'd done what Dad had asked.

So what did she find out as she tried to clear the inn from the project board? Brant Jackson had locked it with his codes, and she could not undo them without his permission. What was supposed to have been a single conversation in one day had dragged on all week. But today she was going to send Ben a message to let him know the contract was dissolved.

The inn was still technically under contract.

Stepping off the elevator, she walked down the hall past Jeremy before he could stop her.

Cami marched into Brant's office with every ounce of experience and courage she could muster. "We need to talk."

Dad stood, gestured to his earpiece, then motioned for Cami to have a seat in one of the tan leather chairs by his desk.

She remained standing. She wanted to be ready for him the moment he ended his call.

"Not what I was looking for, Marv—"

Cami focused her eyes on her dad. He leaned forward. His shoulders drooped. Frustration deepened the lines around his eyes as he pinched the bridge of his nose.

Cami glanced at his walls. Still blank. She'd told him she could get some artwork for him to hang last time she'd been here.

She looked back at her father, and for a moment, she saw the fun, sweet, loving dad of her childhood. The one that had splashed in the pool with her at the inn.

The longing to escape to the inn whispered across her heart again. But next time she visited, a new owner would greet her— once she could get the project unlocked from Akron's systems. The notion made her uneasy.

"Good. Today." Dad was ending his call. "Yes, Hearts Bend."

Cami rolled her shoulders back. Who was he talking to about Hearts Bend? Was this why he'd locked up the inn's file?

When he hung up the phone, he took command of their conversation. "I see things are progressing well in Indy. Did you find an apartment yet?"

"No, but I will. Dad, why is the inn contract locked in the system?" Cami faced him, arms folded, guard up.

"What I want to know is how it got into the system in the first place. I asked you not to buy it."

"Astrid saw the signed contract and loaded it. She knew Ben needed a quick turnaround. By the time I found out, project management had locked it for processing. When I talked with them, they said you locked it. I've told Ben we're not buying it. I need to delete it so he can put it on the market. Why is it still locked?"

"I decided to go ahead with it. We'll close on the fifteenth, and Ben can go back to his real life. I think we'll clear the land and put it up for sale or build something new and modern."

"Why? Why would you do that? The inn is a beloved landmark."

"It's falling apart, under revenue, and has a lien on it from the bank. Time to put up something else."

"If we buy it from Ben, we cannot destroy it. I promised him we would preserve it. You know your reputation in Hearts Bend is to bulldoze everything."

"Shows you how small-town people think. I only wanted to knock down the old Wedding Shop, which was a disaster at the time."

"It's beautiful now. Dad, the inn remains. Either that, or we let it go and Ben sells to the Grangers out of Georgia."

"Last I looked I was still head of this company, Cami."

She lowered her arms and stepped closer to his desk. "Then let's talk about what this is really all about. Mama."

"Don't bring up her name."

"You hate the inn because that's where Mama died and you know you'd let her down—"

"Camellia, I'd watch your words."

"Did you know one of her paintings is in the lobby?"

He didn't answer but turned his back and stared out the window.

"You're not tearing down the inn. Period," Cami said. "I'll resign if you do. I gave my word on behalf of Akron Developments, and that's gold. Isn't that what you're always preaching? So, free up the file, or let me handle this project my way."

Thursday afternoon, Ben read Cami's text.

Dad says to go through with it. We're buying the inn. Do you feel like a yo-yo?

So, the inn was sold to Cami after all. He felt relieved. Cami would love the place like he loved it.

He'd felt like a parent dropping his child off with strangers when he thought of the Georgia couple. It had given him some sense of how his parents had felt leaving him in Hearts Bend with his grandparents. He should cut them some slack. They'd done what they thought was best. His grandparents had been almost as good as being with his mom and dad.

Evening was settling over the grounds when Ben walked from the lobby onto the porch carrying a few tools to return to the barn. Myrtle May was checking in weekend guests, and Walt banged around in the kitchen with his next great tuna recipe.

Ben grinned. He had a sneaking suspicion Walt made the tuna just to mess with Myrtle May.

He walked down the porch steps and along the path to the garden, which was soaked in the setting sunlight. He paused by the lilies. "I could use a bit of your trust in the Almighty."

One of the lilies swayed from side to side as if answering.

Ben continued to the barn. After he'd fixed Room Eight, he'd stored the tools in the office to return to the barn later. Ray hated a messy work bench, so Ben wanted to wait until he had time to put everything in its proper place. He'd left a few tools on the work bench in the barn yesterday that also needed to be put away. As he reached the door, Ray popped out.

"Ray, I thought you'd gone for the day."

"Fixing to head that way now. Had to put someone's tools away." He arched his brow and gazed at Ben.

"I was on my way to clean up, so thank you."

"Find a new buyer for the inn? Listen, son, don't worry about me. If the new owners don't want to keep me on, I'll go on and retire. I'm set for it."

"You're in good hands. Akron is buying the inn. Specifically, Cami."

"Really?" Ray shook his head. "Like I said, I'm all set to retire. I understand you got to do what you got to do."

Ben leaned against the barn. "You sound like you don't approve."

"It's not up to me." Ray looked at Ben, one hand casually in his pocket, the other hanging by his side. Not at all ruffled by Ben's sharp tone. "Did you pray about it?" When Ben didn't answer, Ray went on. "If you don't ask, He can't answer. Ever think He might have something for you better than that fancy place Down Under? That your yellow brick road is right here in Hearts Bend? You can't live your life running from the things you fear or trying to be somebody you've cooked up in your head. You have to be the man God made you to be."

Afraid? Was he afraid? Somewhere in the twilight, a mourning dove cooed a hallowed lament. Ben wasn't afraid to talk to God. But why bother Him when Ben already had a great plan for his life?

In Ben's experience, God had a way of changing a man's plans, and he wasn't a hundred percent on board with that right now.

"Don't be like your great-great-uncle Ned," Ray said. "He collected all sorts of grand stuff from around the world with the intent of building a hotel and a home right here in HB. He spent thousands when the estates were failing in England.

Bought all sorts of rare antique pieces. You know what he did with it all?"

"Well, since there's no big hotel or fine house in town, I'm guessing nothing."

"Yup, packed a lot of the stuff in this barn. The rest, all that gorgeous furniture, burned when the old warehouse went up in flames in '38."

"I'm not Great-Great-Uncle Ned. I'm not acquiring and not building. I'm doing something with my *stuff*, as you put it."

"You're missing the point, son. Your uncle Ned was looking for happiness in grand things, in money. But none of it made him happy. That's what I'm asking you, Ben. Are you happy?"

The question struck an exposed nerve. Ben had never asked himself that question, but suddenly his entire body resonated with it.

Of course he was happy. He was living his dream. He was successful.

But *was* he happy?

Ray nodded a good evening but after a few steps turned back. "Your granddaddy always used to sit at his desk with the door closed when he talked to God. Nine times out of ten, he came out with an answer. If not, he emerged with peace, believing God was taking care of him and your granny."

Ben watched Ray walk away and stayed there, leaning against the barn wall until he had to follow the inn's lights back to the porch. Guests filled the dining area, and the part-time girl, Lori, was taking orders.

Inside the office, Ben closed the door, then sat at his grandfather's desk. The only light was that of the small desk lamp.

Bowing his head, he prayed, feeling every bit like one of the lilies in Ray's garden, trusting God to take care of him and show him the way.

CHAPTER 13

Five days had passed since Cami had sent Ben a text—not that she was counting. She settled into her seat inside the Frothy Monkey in downtown Nashville with her sister across from her for a latte and Danish. As they finished their chat, Annalise's phone rang with a Vicki Carmichael song.

The moment Annalise answered, the singer began to cry.

"...spilled the beans...media everywhere...cancelled...two weeks away...wedding."

The more Vicki went on, the more pale Annalise became. "Okay...okay...don't worry. We'll work it out, we'll work it out."

Annalise hung up and started for the parking lot. "Someone went to the media and revealed the location of the wedding. Vicki canceled her contract with the Oasis. The media is all over the place."

Cami cleared the table of their trash and hurried out to meet Annalise, who stood next to the car.

"How can people be so heartless?" Annalise said. "Obviously, it's a breach of the non-disclosure, but now she needs a new wedding venue. Worse yet, this 'source' has labeled her a bridezilla. She's not, and I feel bad I painted her that way in the beginning. She's just a bride wanting the wedding of her dreams."

Annalise got in the passenger seat while Cami slid behind the wheel. "You're the best wedding planner in Nashville—"

"I'm not, but thank you."

"You'll find something."

"In two weeks? It's going to be close to impossible."

"Can she postpone?"

Annalise looked over at Cami. "Would you want to?"

If Cami found the right guy, she wouldn't want anything to stand in her way. "Good point." Cami turned out of the parking lot and headed down Avenue South.

"She's looking for a location as well, but friends and family have already booked reservations. Cami, I'm gonna need your help."

Cami slowed at the traffic light and peered at her sister. "Anything you need. Consider it my parting gift."

"I take back everything I ever said about you."

"Ha, no you don't. Now, where can we have a lovely wedding in two weeks?"

Annalise jumped in her seat, stretching against the seat belt. "That's it! You know the perfect location. Vicki will love it. The inn, Cami, the inn. Why didn't I think of this sooner?"

The light turned green, and Cami stomped on the gas. The inn? Annalise was right, the inn was perfect, but Cami was not ready to see Ben.

They'd had their goodbye. She wanted to hang onto the sweetness of his final kiss. Seeing him would remind her all over again they'd never have more than a fleeting summer romance.

"The inn is perfect. Even if it does need a bit of fixing up."

Annalise was on her phone. "Vicki will die for the rustic, hometown charm. There, hit I-65 and head to Hearts Bend. Vicki, I found the perfect place. No, no, I'm not going to tell you until I visit the property. I'll call you later."

"Cami, call Ben. Tell him we want access to the barn and everything. When are you closing on the place?"

"The fifteenth."

"The wedding is on the nineteenth, so it will be your property by the time of the wedding, so I don't think he'll object."

But I object! She didn't want to see Ben. She feared her heart would decide to fall in love at a glance.

Next to her, Annalise was making a list on her phone. "The barn is perfect for pictures. So country music. Right on brand with Vicki's music. How's the pond? If it's not clean, we can get it cleaned up."

"It's clean."

"Look at this, God is providing for Vicki through me. What do you say to that? Why aren't you calling Ben?"

"Nope. I can't call Ben." Still, Cami merged onto I-65 toward Hearts Bend.

"Why not?" Annalise pulled Cami's hand over the center console and laid it on her stomach. Wait, did she feel a tiny hint of a bump? "Not even for the baby?"

Cami swerved as she twisted toward her sister, and everything clicked into place. The bags under her eyes, the nausea, the weight loss, the happiness when she mentioned Steve, then suddenly looking bright and glowy. "You're pregnant?"

"Yes, I am, Auntie Cami. So you have to help me. I'm already running on fumes. Who knew being pregnant was a full-time job in and of itself? There is no tired like pregnant tired."

Excitement coursed through Cami. A baby. "Why didn't you tell me?"

"I was afraid of miscarriage. I had a scare really early on with some spotting. Steve's sister miscarried four times, so we didn't want to share the news until week thirteen."

"Oh, Annalise! Just when I'm moving away! I'll never forgive you for this." But her tears were mixed with laughter. Finally, a baby in the family.

"So will you call Ben?" Annalise patted her middle.

Cami commanded her phone to call Ben Carter. "You're shameless, Annalise, using your kid this way. How many times are you going to use your child to get your way?"

"From here on out, Aunt Cami. From here on out."

Cami laughed just as Ben answered her call. "Ben, how about some company?"

Ben had thought seeing Cami would be awkward, but like always, he felt peace in her presence. When she and Annalise arrived, she was a bit formal and standoffish, but once they started touring the grounds, her stiff persona faded.

"You made this sound like it would be an intimate wedding." Ben walked with Cami as they surveyed the small field next to the inn. Her sister stood in the shade of the inn, sketching on her iPad.

"It is. There will only be about seventy people, and I think this field will be perfect. We'll set up a tent and chairs."

"Seventy people? Cami, they're not all going to fit."

"Sure they will. We'll have the altar here." Cami walked forward and stretched her arms out. "An arch, with twinkle lights. The folding chairs will go..." Cami took several steps and stopped. "Here."

Ben surveyed the area again. She was right. It would fit, with room to spare. He had a lot of experience with weddings and receptions, corporate events and parties, but they'd all taken place on a VJR property, which had a separate event staff.

"The cloth runner could start here, under another arch." Cami gestured her arms to show the arch, and for one moment, Ben could see it. The arches, the chairs, the runner, even the bride in a white dress. But the bride walking toward him was the woman he saw in front of him. Her dark curls hanging over one shoulder, a bouquet of Tennessee wildflowers in her hands, and a smile meant just for him.

"Cami, it's perfect." Annalise waved from the shade. "Vicki loves it. I sent some mockups to her along with some pictures. I bet she—" Annalise's phone rang. "That's her now."

"Ben, thank you for letting us descend on you like this."

"No problem. It'll be your property by the time of the wedding. I'll do what I can to help, but after the closing, I really must head down to Sydney."

The talk was so formal and cordial, as if they'd never had any feelings. Cami started down the future center aisle, and Ben fell in step with her.

"How have you been?" He tucked a loose curl behind her ear. Her dark eyes looked up into his, searching. She stepped back and secured the curl he'd just touched.

"Busy with Indy. I sold my place, but I'm hiring a packer and movers. Working on ideas for the inn renovations. And oh, Annalise just told me I'm going to be an aunt."

Ben glanced to where Annalise sat on the porch steps laughing and charming Vicki. "I thought she glowed a little. Congratulations."

"Thanks." She leaned closer. "I am banking on a girl, but I know Steve will be pronouncing the baby a boy."

She laughed, and Ben loved the carefree feeling it invoked.

"Hey," she said, grabbing his hand then letting go. "Sorry for all the mix-up about the inn. I will be overseeing the project. I walked into Dad's office and told him this place was mine to manage. He relented, albeit grudgingly."

"I appreciate that, Cami. I trust you." Ben looked toward the crooked, faded shutters and the roof that needed new shingles. "Do you really think an up-and-coming singer will want to get married out here?"

"Of course. What's not to love about this place, Ben? The exposure will help the inn and—"

"Darn, I should've locked in on a higher sale price."

"If it were up to me, I would offer you more. I did add covering the bank loan into the deal, so I guess I did offer more."

"It's all good. What means more than the money is that you will be the inn's guardian angel. Granddaddy and Granny are smiling down from heaven."

"Great news!" Annalise approached with her arms wide. "Vicki loved the pictures and the sketches I sent her. She's requested we book all the available rooms for family and the wedding party. Most of the guests have booked Nashville hotels. They can just drive over for the day. The caterer is on her way to check out the facility. She'll need access to the kitchen, Ben."

He looked at Cami just as she turned to him. "Walt," they said in unison.

"Maybe give him the day off," Cami said.

"Or the entire week."

"This is going to be perfect." Annalise let out a big sigh. Her dark eyes, so like Cami's, smiling. "Thank you, Ben! Vicki wanted to know where to send the deposit money."

"What deposit money? Have we decided on a price?"

"Fifty thousand was my estimation. Is that enough?"

Ben choked. "Fifty grand for this place?"

"Well, you are going to have to pretty it up with some paint and clean up the grounds a bit. But yes, fifty thousand."

"Um, tell her to send it to the inn's PayPal." Ben rattled off the email address, feeling a bit like he'd stepped into an alternate reality. "And for fifty grand, I'll have this place spit shined and ready for inspection."

"Ben," Cami said, "let me offer some Akron resources. After all, the inn will be ours at the time of the wedding."

"Thank you, but let me do this for Granny. She loved having weddings here, and I think this is the perfect send-off from one family to another."

Cami's eyes glistened. "I am so going to miss you," she whispered.

"Ditto," he said.

Cami's phone rang. She glanced at the screen. "Indy's calling." She wandered off as she answered her phone.

He wasn't ready to go. His mind told him to let go, but his heart kept hanging on. He'd be fine once he was back on the job.

He'd been praying more, sitting at Granddaddy's desk. He'd actually started to sense a presence.

Okay, God, I'm listening.

"Ben." Annalise stepped closer and lowered her voice. "Vicki loves the cottages and wants to use the larger one as a sort of bride's suite. It's Cottage Three." She glanced back at Cami. "I told her I wasn't sure. I don't want to upset Cami."

"What about you?"

"I miss my mother every day, but I wasn't here when she died. I seldom stayed in the cottage, so it doesn't bother me as much."

"It needs some work, but I'll fix it if that's what the bride wants. But please tell Cami, okay? I wouldn't want her blindsided."

"You love her, don't you?"

"Have a nice evening, Annalise," Ben said. "I'll see you next week."

CHAPTER 14

Wedding plans, the inn's repair, and preparation for Cami's move to Indy melded together as the next several days flew by.

"Thanks for the update, Matthew. I'll have Astrid call you, and she can pick out the new flooring." Cami hung up from the video call with the Indy construction manager. The humid breeze lifted her hair and only slightly combated the heat. Cami had set up outside the inn under a pool umbrella for the call.

She'd known it wouldn't be good news the moment the contractor had reached out. The flooring that had been selected for the new office in Indy had been lost in shipping. They could reorder it, but it wouldn't come in until after September first, and he wouldn't be back to finish up the flooring and final details until mid-November.

However, Matthew had found new flooring options that were in stock at a local lumberyard. Cami sent Astrid a text to get with Matthew about the details.

If another trip to Indianapolis was required, she'd have to go. If it was too close to the wedding, Astrid could probably handle it on her own.

The last few days had been packed full of juggling work-related issues, calls with Max about apartment leases, and a million messages from Annalise about wedding details.

Every time Cami complained about how much her sister was relying on her, Annalise would touch her belly and say, "Baby needs help," and next thing Cami knew, she was elbows deep in tulle, flowers, lights, food, and guest lists.

What made everything worth it was the trips to Hearts Bend. It was in the small town where, even in the midst of all the busyness, Cami could breathe.

Picking up a large basket of solar lights, she headed toward Cottage Three. Annalise had dropped the news that Vicki wanted to use the place to dress and be with her bridesmaids.

Cami braced for the sense of loss, of missing her mother, but instead she felt a bit of joy.

"Mama would love for a bride and her party to redeem the space where she died."

But as she pushed the lights into soft dirt on the path leading up to *the* cottage, emotions ran through her.

Never mind the August afternoon was sweltering. Sweat dripped down her back as she worked. When she arrived at Cottage Three, she rose up and studied the robin's-egg-blue door. Mama had gone to the paint store with Mrs. Carter and picked out the paint color. Cami and Ben had tagged along and enjoyed ice cream afterward.

Ben had replaced the windows, and the glass sparkled in the light. The window boxes contained fresh, colorful flowers, courtesy of Ray.

The cottage looked the way she remembered it—minus

Mama's paint boots sitting just outside the door. She'd always wanted a pair of boots just like Mama's.

Cami grabbed another solar light out of the basket and jammed it into the dirt at the edge of the little stoop. Now to add lights to the rest of the garden.

"Annalise said you were lighting the path." Ben's deep voice shouldn't have surprised her. He'd sought her out every evening when she arrived after work to help her sister.

A simple conversation, a gentle press against her back, a whispered word in her ear. Cami did her best to keep it casual. Nothing deep. Nothing emotional. Nothing lasting.

But her skin always tingled at his touch, and her heartbeat tripled its tempo when she caught sight of him.

"These lights arrived. I thought I'd help with the garden." He held up an Amazon box. "Where did you leave off?"

"Here." She gestured to the robin's-egg-blue door. "At Mama's door."

"How's it feel to be standing here? Where you *left off* fifteen years ago?"

She shrugged. "I'm not sure. I think she'd love that a wedding was taking place here. She'd love that the door she painted was still blue."

"I think she'd love that you were standing here," Ben said. He stepped ahead of her with a gentle touch on her arm. "I'll go in with you if you want."

Go in? Really? She began to tremble "I don't know."

"What are you afraid of?"

"The truth. That it's my fault she died. I didn't get her help in time."

"It's not your fault, Cami. I know you know that."

"In my head, yes, but in here..." She tapped over her heart. "I wonder if there's some truth to it."

Ben took the basket of lights from her and set it on the ground. "Come on, let's go in together."

For a flash second, she was ten and chasing Ben around the cottage. Granny Carter walked Mama to the front door and gave her the key.

We're so happy you're with us again. Ben, be a good host and take Cami inside for some cookies.

She took a step, then hesitated. Her gaze mixed with Ben's. She was not alone. Not this time.

Cami stepped onto the whitewashed step she used to sit on with Mama and watch the fireflies.

At the blue door, she remembered the night when Ben had walked her home—after they'd fallen out of the tree house—and, holding hands, bid each other a shy goodbye.

Here he stood with her again. He pushed the door open. "When you're ready."

"I feel like I'm standing in an igloo," she said with a shaky laugh.

"Nerves."

Cami took a trembling step inside and waited, listening, feeling. She felt Ben's presence next to her. The walls and the dark wood cabinets in the kitchen had been repainted a simple white, and new hardwood had been added throughout. The furniture was new—a beautifully simple gray couch and new curtains had been added.

"It's peaceful," she said. "I thought it'd feel like death, full of sadness and tears."

"But that wasn't your mama, was it? She left her joy and peace here."

Cami wiped away the tears spilling down her cheeks. "She did, didn't she."

"Maybe she left them here for you."

"So buying the inn was her plan all along?" She laughed at his supernatural suggestion, but deep down, it gave her confidence. "Ben, I'm going to turn this inn into something we'd all be proud of. You, me, Mama, your parents and grandparents, and everyone who called the inn home for a night or a week or a month."

Suddenly, Mama's sweet voice whispered across her heart.

'Tis so sweet to trust in Jesus... Just to rest upon His promise... O, for grace to trust Him more.

Just as Cami started to sing, so did Ben. When they finished the song together, tears were streaming down his cheeks as well as hers.

It was then she fully knew she could trust her heart to Jesus.

"Come on," Cami said, wiping the last of her tears and pointing to the furniture dropped off but not arranged. "Let's get this place in order."

Together they moved the pieces into place. The couch against the outside wall, a small white coffee table centered in front of it. Cami found a vase in the kitchen and arranged some flowers from the garden in it.

"The walls are a bit bare," Cami said.

"Come see the artwork I found in the barn." Ben moved to a box along the wall and pulled out a large painting of a red camellia.

"Oh my." Cami's breath caught when she saw the piece. The familiar strokes, the details that had taken hours to get just so. The dew on the petals, the shadows to give depth.

"Do you like it?" Ben sounded like he knew he'd found a buried treasure.

"Yes." Cami stepped closer, lifting her hand to feel the textures she knew so well. She'd memorized this painting, done it several times. In fact, if she was willing to bet, she'd guess there were a few more variations of this painting in the box—ones in pink, white, purple, and blue. But the red was her favorite.

"This is mine." Her voice sounded husky even to her own ears. She'd spent an entire summer working on these paintings—picking the flower Mama had named her after. She'd been fascinated by the strength, the dignity she'd found within the petals.

"Yours?" Ben looked back at the picture. "I thought you took all of yours home. They're incredible."

"Mama was teaching me the technique. I can see all my amateur mistakes, but you know, there's an innocence about it." Cami took the picture from Ben and held it in the sunlight coming through the southern window. The light played across the painting Mama had spent hours showing her how to shade, how to add depth and texture to. "I feel like I've found a lost piece of myself, Ben. Thank you."

Thank God.

Ben pulled out a few more paintings and leaned them against the wall. "Maybe you should start painting again?"

"Maybe." Cami set the painting down and looked at another. She'd not wanted to see the details anymore. To consider the One who made all the little things for her to enjoy. "I got busy after college, and it didn't seem as important. I wasn't really keeping Mama alive by trying to become her. Dad said I was good in business, so I followed him."

"Do you want to take these pictures home with you?"

Cami shook her head. "No, let's hang them in the cottage."

Ben pulled out another painting. "Look, this one's not finished."

Cami covered her mouth. The bold strokes, the blending colors, the flowers, and the penciled outline of a barn. "That was Mama's. That was the painting she was working on when..."

The lump in her throat cut off words. She shook her head.

"We, um, we'd spent the afternoon in the garden. We set up our easels, and I finished one of the camellias—I can't remember which one. Mama had drafted that scene on a previous trip, and she started painting it that day she died. We were going to a movie, then dinner at Ella's."

Ben set the painting aside and wrapped his arms around Cami. She didn't resist but leaned into him.

His hand stroked her hair. "I'm sorry, Cami. There are so many memories here."

"Please don't be." Cami looked up at his face. "You helped me remember the good, and I really need that."

"You really are very talented. You should paint for yourself. And for the Emerald. I'd hang it in the lobby and tell everyone it's from a new, high-end artist."

She laughed. "I'll never be that person, and I won't open a studio like I dreamed when I was young. Dreams change, but this has been good for me. I cut out a part of myself after Mama died. Now that we have the inn, I'll come back as much as I can to pick up those lost pieces."

And to remember that she could trust God, who created all the beauty in the world around her.

Ben's hand cupped her cheek, his thumb drawing soft circles, and she let him search her eyes, her soul. She had nothing to hide. If he saw love there, so be it. She wasn't afraid anymore.

She'd given up on love in this room, and now, in the arms of the man she loved, she'd finally found what she'd lost. Peace. Trust. Hope.

Cami roped her arms about his neck and rose up on her toes, inviting him to kiss her. She hoped he'd accept.

Without any hesitation, he covered her lips with his and kissed until she floated away.

Only one more shutter. Climbing the ladder, Ben loosened its screws and carried it down, sweat running into his eyes, down his face and neck. Five days until closing. He was determined to finish repairing, painting, and rehanging the shutters before then. On the ground, he set the shutter against the side of the inn, removed his ball cap, and wiped his forehead. Done. With this part. This wedding was getting the inn in shape.

"Yoohoo! Benji!" Myrtle May stood on the front steps of the inn, waving and holding a large glass of sweet iced tea. Bart trailed behind her, his tail wagging happily.

Bless her. Ben closed the ladder and laid it on its side before heading in her direction. One of the guests had little kids, and Ben had seen the youngest tyke climbing a tree. The ladder might be too tempting.

"On Christ, the solid Rock, I stand, all other ground is sinking sand." Myrtle May's voice was even more off-key today, and she seemed distracted as she handed him the glass.

"It's hotter than hades out here today, boy. You haven't come in to drink near enough." She'd started looking out for him as soon as he'd arrived in Hearts Bend after Granny had passed, and as the weeks went on, she became more and more motherly. Who would look out for him in Sydney? He'd miss being around family. He'd miss Myrtle May.

Sitting on the side of the porch, he looked out over the grounds. Cami had sent down a crew to help with the landscaping. Ray had bristled at first, but then realized the team of four had accomplished more trimming and pulling than he had in the last so many years.

"Just leave my lilies alone," he'd said. His garden was the one thing he kept weeded and beautiful. "That patch of ground is my heart."

The field had been mowed and was ready for chairs and a tent. Another field was being prepped for the reception. Annalise and Cami combed over the property almost every evening.

The floors in the cottages and rooms had been sanded and polished. All the bed and bathroom linens were new, and the inn was starting to smile, to feel loved.

Ben's thoughts drifted to the sweet kisses he'd shared with Cami in Cottage Three a few days ago. He never wanted to let her go. In fact, that sentiment was becoming more and more dominant. Doubts about leaving floated through him throughout the day as he saw the inn start to shine.

But that was ridiculous. He had a contract with Viridian. He had one to sell the place to Akron. Signed, sealed, delivered. Done. He was just being sentimental.

He drank the last of his tea and carried the glass inside, grabbing one of Walt's tuna sandwiches on his way out. They weren't half bad. He didn't know what Myrtle May went on and on about.

Stepping onto the porch, he was about to go fetch the shutters when a sleek black Mercedes pulled into the inn parking lot. A well-dressed man with salt-and-pepper hair stepped out. He was tall and athletic with an air of confidence.

Brant Jackson. No one needed to tell Ben. He knew.

"Well, I'll be." The screen door clapped behind Myrtle May. "After all this time."

"Brant Jackson."

"One and the same." Myrtle May smoothed her hand down her purple-and-red skirt, fidgeted with her dazzling bright-teal top, then fluffed her hair. "Wow, he's a hunk of man, but I'm going inside to take Bart out the back door."

"You running scared, Myrtle May?"

"Darn right. Like Adam and Eve should've been afraid of that snake in the garden. He's a charmer, that one. I'll either melt in a puddle at his feet or give him a piece of my mind, and he ain't worth it. However, I was reminded this morning that I should watch my tongue, and I aim to prove some cranky old man wrong."

Cranky old man? Walt. Only he could get so far under Myrtle May's skin.

Ben stepped off the porch and met the great Brant Jackson in the yard. Brant was precise in his movements, pausing to study the inn and the surroundings. Ben could see Cami in his profile and lean frame.

"Mr. Jackson," Ben said, offering his hand. "I'm Ben Carter."

"I've come to see what my daughters are raving about." He didn't shake Ben's hand. "Cami insists this property is special." He sounded dubious.

Ben raised his guard. This didn't feel like a friendly visit. "I appreciate that Cami saw the value in my inn."

"It's Akron's now."

"Almost. We've not closed yet."

"I hear you're fixing her up for a wedding."

"Yes, the one Annalise is planning." Ben walked with Brant toward the house. Without the shutters, the windows looked naked and alone.

Brant made his way into the inn. "I'd like to look around."

Ben pressed his fist against his chest. Somehow Brant's appearance made the sale of the inn a stark reality.

This place would no longer be his. His home base. No more Granddaddy and Granny or holiday dinners. No more cozy winter nights by the fireplace or summer barbecues. No more Hearts Bend.

Ben eased through the inn's screen door. The front desk and dog bed were empty. Myrtle May hadn't been kidding around. Brant paused in the center of the lobby, but he seemed lost in another world. After a moment he stepped around the reception desk and stood under his wife's painting.

He started to raise his hand to the canvas but hesitated, cleared his throat, and stepped back.

"Granny always said it was yours," Ben said, propping himself against the wall down to the hall, arms folded. "Macie painted it for you."

"I don't mean to contradict your granny," Brant said, "but Macie painted this for you. Well, you and Cami. It's hanging here because she wanted it to hang here." He reached for the painting and brushed his hand over the couple on the bench. "That ole bench. Do you still have it?"

"Not sure. Maybe buried in the barn."

"We spent a lot of time on that bench, talking and dreaming. Planning." Brant's voice faded. "Then the business took off, and I lost track of what was important. Lost the little dreams and the quiet moments with my wife and girls. No, she painted that picture after she'd had a dream."

The man fell quiet, studying the painting, lost in his memories. Ben moved back quietly. He wasn't sure how he felt about the man. His success aside, he didn't appear to be very fatherly to his daughter. Cami seemed to carry some sort of burden related to him.

Ben started toward his office but stopped when Brant spoke again. "In the dream, she and I were old, empty nesters. We came back to the inn to visit Cami and you. She felt God was saying you'd be married one day." His laugh was full of sentiment. "But she never wanted to say anything to influence either of you. She said God could handle matchmaking. She painted the two of you on the bench as a promise to her own heart. When and if you married, she'd reveal the truth."

"So why are you telling me now?" Ben moved closer to the painting. He was the man on the bench with Cami? Yes, please. Something was happening to him. Something he could not control, but it felt so freeing.

"I don't know. I guess I thought you needed to know. You're headed to Australia, and she's going to Indianapolis."

"Do we need the bench for this dream to come true? 'Cause I'm not sure we can find it."

"I don't think the bench matters so much as the people on it." Brant glanced around the inn. "Does Macie have other paintings here?"

"No, but Cami has a few."

"Show me."

"They're in Cottage Three, sir."

Brant nodded once. "Then perhaps I'll leave it for now."

"I have one of Cami's paintings in my office here. It was my favorite."

The red camellia leaned against the wall behind the desk. He wanted to ship it to Sydney, but he couldn't bring himself to do it.

As Brant approached the picture, Ben knew he wouldn't be the one to keep the painting.

"I have no right to ask, but can I—" Brant knelt in front of the canvas.

"It's yours," Ben said.

"Thank you."

The sage businessman didn't stick around much longer. As Ben watched him drive away, he had an overwhelming desire to pray for him.

And for the first time in years, that inner peace that Granny had always talked about, that Dad mentioned so often, flooded over Ben. The peace that only a heavenly Father could give.

He also had some really new information. Macie Jackson had dreamed that he married Cami? It had been such a reality to her she'd painted a picture of their future.

Now for the million-dollar question. Did Ben tell Cami?

CHAPTER 15

*T*wo days later, Ben climbed the ladder for the last time. The shutters were repaired, painted, and rehung.

As he stored the ladder in the barn, Aunt Myrtle May yoohooed for him again. She stood on the porch with a glass of tea. He'd just downed the entire thing when a white Ford F-150 rumbled toward the inn.

Two men exited the truck, talking and laughing, stopping at the truck bed to grab tool belts and tools.

"Those boys look to be far from home." Myrtle May gestured at the men and called for Bart to follow her. "I'm going inside, but you holler for me or Walt if you need backup."

Ben handed Myrtle May his empty glass as she passed, then went to meet the men. "How can I help you today?"

The older man lifted his clipboard and glanced over the paper. "I'm Dean Wicker. Akron Development hired us to do an environmental study. Need to see how many buildings they can put on here."

"Excuse me?" The ground shifted beneath Ben, a personal earthquake. "Akron hired you? To do an environmental study?"

"Test the soil and water so when they knock this place down—"

"Dean, I'm Ben Carter, the owner. Akron does not own this place." Not yet anyway.

"Says here they do."

"We haven't closed yet."

"Don't know about that, but we got our orders."

"Look, can you just give me a minute?" Ben pulled out his phone. "Let me make a call."

Had he been a complete fool? All that mushy sentiment from Brant and how Macie had dreamed about him and Cami. And where was Cami on this? She'd promised she would protect the inn from her father. They'd not even closed, and Brant had sent an environmental crew.

Cami's phone rang without an answer. So he left her a message. "Cami, it's me, Ben. Call me. It's important." He hit End and turned back to the men. "Listen, you'll just have to come back later."

"Not until we get a call from someone at Akron."

Ben started for the barn. He'd sort of liked Brant Jackson the other day as he'd waxed about the past. He'd given him Cami's painting. But Brant had just been on a scouting mission. Seeing what he could put over on Ben. Cami would be powerless to stop him.

Ben felt like the kid his parents had dropped off in Hearts Bend, promising they'd return for him in the summer. But he'd never lived in Papua New Guinea again. Not until after college.

His phone buzzed with a call from Cami. "Hey, sorry I missed your call. What's wrong? You sounded upset."

"You promised." He didn't bother to moderate his voice.

"You promised to protect the inn. You weren't going to let your dad destroy this place."

"He's not going to destroy the inn. Ben, what's going on?"

"Two environmental surveyors showed up to take soil samples. Akron hired them. Said that Akron was going to tear down the inn." Ben paced in frustration. Did he have a big L on his forehead?

"Ben, slow down. What are you talking about? Dad hired an environmental team?"

"Dean Wicker."

"Dean? Oh, Ben, I'm sure this is a misunderstanding."

"The misunderstanding is that you thought you could control your father. Cami, he can do whatever he wants without telling you, especially if you're in another state. And here I thought he was kind of nice when he showed up here the other day."

"He showed up at the inn?"

"Yes. Was our relationship just a ploy for Akron to get its claws into Hearts Bend?"

"Ben." Cami's whispered voice broke. "There's no ploy, I promise. I'm not out to get you or the inn. I can't believe you'd think that about me."

"It's clear you cannot protect this place from your dad." He knew what he had to do. "I want out of the deal." The words came out like a sword and dagger.

"Are you serious? What about Sydney?" Her sweet voice oozed with compassion and concern, but why should she care? The tenderness only added fuel to the anger burning inside Ben.

"I'll figure it out, but the deal is off." He'd have Mr. Graham look over the contract, find a loophole.

A beat. Two. "If that's really what you want, Ben, fine. I'll cancel the contract. I won't be able to pay the earnest money since—"

"I don't care about the money. Just make it happen." Ben ended the call before she said something else in her calm, tender tone. She sounded sincere. She sounded hurt.

He found Dean and his man walking the property and taking pictures. "There's been a change of plans. The deal is off, and Akron won't be purchasing this property. You can leave now."

Dean reached up and scratched at his hair under his ball cap, then pulled the bill back down. "I told you someone from Akron needs to call." His phone pinged, and he glanced at it. "I guess you're right." He held up the phone to show an Akron number. "Have a good day."

When they'd gone, Ben made his way to the pond. Man, he probably owed Cami an apology. He hadn't realized how much being left here as a kid had defined him.

If anyone lied to him or put one over on him, he never trusted them again. But he should call Cami, try to work things out. He lifted his phone, but before he could call her, Jordan rang.

"G'day," Ben said. "It's early there. Please tell me you have good news."

"We need a new head of housekeeping. Jenna resigned. Her husband has been transferred to Perth. I've listed it but wanted to keep you in the loop."

Sirens sounded in the distance, growing closer.

"Can we promote someone under Jenna?"

"We have a few who want to apply. I think we can fill the position from in-house. Ben, the place is looking amazing. You won't believe the progress since you were here."

"You deserve all the credit."

The sirens cut off, and Ben focused on finishing up the call.

"Oh, there's one more thing, Ben. The men's sauna isn't functioning, and the company is sending a replacement, but it won't be here until after we open."

"Send the information. I'll try to speed things up." He hung up and headed for the kitchen. He needed another iced tea and a cookie. And to make sure the sirens didn't herald more bad news.

He bumped into the fire chief and an electrician. "What's going on here?"

Walt, wrapped in his big, stained apron, stepped around the chief. "Just a small fire. Nothing to worry you about."

"Except I'm shutting down the kitchen," the chief said. "The electrical is out of code, and your appliances are at the end of life. Between the two, you're lucky this place didn't burn to the ground years ago."

"Are you shutting us down? We're hosting a big wedding next week."

"You can still have guests, but you won't be serving any meals from this kitchen until the wiring is updated and the appliances replaced."

Ben thanked the chief and the electrician, then turned to Walt. "Please don't tell me you knew about this."

"Okay, I won't tell you."

"He knew," Myrtle May said. "So did your Granny. It was in that inspector report."

How could Ben have forgotten about that? Why hadn't he done something about it? Ben headed to the coffee bar and poured a cup of Walt's rock-gut. They'd formed a conspiracy. Granny, Walt, Cami, Jim and Jordan, Ray, the bullfrog who sang outside his basement window every morning at five. God. Surely He was involved somehow.

He stepped into the office and slammed the door before sitting at the desk, trying to shed his frustration. He could use the money from the wedding to cover the rewiring and the new appliances. Then what?

He could call Stan at the bank and try for a refi. He'd need to pay something, but maybe he'd use some of the wedding money to ease a bit of the debt.

Or, or, or... He wanted to talk to Cami. He needed her advice and friendship. But he'd just called her a liar, and maybe he should give her time to cool off. Give himself time to cool off.

He sat at Granddaddy's desk. "Okay, God, what do I do now?"

Ben squeezed his eyes as if it might aid his spiritual hearing. After a few moments when he heard nothing, he reached for his phone.

"Mr. Graham, Akron fell through. I need a buyer for the inn."

Unbelievable. Cami stared at the phone in her hand. She wanted to call Ben back, but he'd sounded so upset. As the packers moved about her, she tried to analyze this call from Ben.

This was Dad with Mama's death all over again. Ben blamed her for something she hadn't done. She hadn't called Dean and his team. But if Ben wanted to blame her, then he could take himself to Sydney without so much as a goodbye.

Except she'd have to see him for Vicki's wedding. What she really needed to do was have it out with Dad. What was he up to now? If he hated the inn, if it reminded him of everything he'd lost, why had he kept it in the system?

Meanwhile, the new condo owners wanted to move in this week, so she had to move out. She'd thought she'd have to put things in storage, but Max had called two days ago with the perfect downtown Indy apartment, and she'd signed the lease.

The movers were going to move her into her new place. She'd unpack when she got there. In the meantime, she'd sleep in Annalise's spare room.

Standing in the middle of her living room, a burly man wrapped a glass sculpture she'd picked up at an art fair with Annalise three summers ago.

She felt hot and stuffy, overwhelmed, and in need of a quiet place to think.

A shatter arrested the movement in the room as the man wrapping the figurine dropped it. Shards scattered across the hardwood.

"I'm sorry, ma'am." The foreman made a note on his clipboard. "Mike, get this cleaned up. Was it a special piece?"

She shook her head, tears budding. "Just the reminder of a fun summer with my sister."

The figurine was a symbol of her life. Shattering.

A couple of men hoisted the couch as Cami wandered down the hall, passing empty rooms. In the spare room where she'd kept her shoes, she closed the door and sat in the middle of the empty space.

Only a few pairs had been moved to Annalise's last night. The rest would travel with the movers. Her new place was downtown in a "highly sought-after area" and within walking distance to shopping and restaurants and a coffee shop. Astrid had also found an apartment in the same complex.

The place needed a bit of work, but she liked the idea of putting her stamp on her new place.

Beyond the walls and door, she heard the movers hauling off her Nashville life, but she had to sort out why Ben blamed her for the mix-up with Dean. His angry words sank deeper with each remembrance. At least she'd been able to text Dean to stop the work.

Cami's phone rang from her shorts pocket, and Astrid's face flashed on the screen.

"Hey, have you checked your email?"

"No, why?" Cami immediately switched her phone to speaker and opened her email. "By the way, I need you to nullify the Hearts Bend Inn contract."

"You're kidding, right?"

"Send the paperwork to the project team. No earnest money payout."

"What happened?"

Dad happened. "I'll tell you when I see you."

Cami skimmed her email. There was a new message from Dad at the top of her inbox. The subject line: Congratulations, Geoffrey Swanson.

Cami closed her eyes and exhaled. "Please tell me this isn't what I think it is."

Astrid sighed over the speaker. "I wish. Brant announced that Geoff was moving to Indianapolis as second-in-command. I hadn't heard any chatter about this around the water cooler. Took me by surprise."

Geoffrey Swanson was a brownnoser who pretended to be a team player but made everything about him. A team win was a Geoffrey win. Shoot, the last time they'd had cupcakes in the staff meeting, he'd taken the last chocolate when he knew it was Cami's favorite. Later, when she'd walked by the room, she'd seen more than half of it in the trash.

Dad knew how she felt about Geoffrey, and he hadn't even asked her about this move. Typical Brant Jackson.

"Thanks for the heads-up, Astrid. I have to go." Cami fell back on the floor and read through the email again. "Second-in-command..."

Dad didn't believe in her. He'd never believe in her. So why employ her? Why send her to Indianapolis? Why dangle the vice president position? He'd just all but announced to the entire company he was sending Geoffrey to keep an eye on Cami.

If she'd hired Geoff, then she'd have made the announcement. But the email had come from the president's office.

"He's punishing me, isn't he? Because I was there when Mama died and couldn't save her. So for the rest of my life, he's going to punish me."

Oh, she really wanted to talk to Ben right now. She missed his wisdom and friendship. She knew what Annalise would say. *He's not punishing you.* But it sure felt like he was.

She had options. She could put in her résumé at their rival firm, Wilson & Co. John Wilson had been wooing her for three years. But darn it, she couldn't do it to Dad. She couldn't betray him or Akron.

She could move to Indianapolis as planned and be the best director Akron Development had ever seen. Show the whole company she didn't need Geoffrey Swanson watching her every move.

She closed her fists and opened them, her fingers itching to move, to hold something.

She wanted to paint.

Was that why Mama had always painted? Had she been dealing with the aftermath of being married to *the* Brant Jackson and all his shenanigans? If Dad had tried to pull stunts like this on Mama, it wasn't a wonder she'd escaped to Hearts Bend so often.

A knock sounded on the door. "Ma'am. We're all done here."

Cami signed the paperwork and walked the mover out. One lone box remained in the corner. The box she'd brought back from the inn last week. The one with Mama's unfinished painting.

She took a few deep breaths and one final walk through of her home. The remodeled master bath, the new hardwood floors. Everything reflected Cami and her taste.

No wonder nothing in Indy felt right. It wasn't. The places were sterile. She hadn't picked all the finishing pieces. She'd be back in Nashville someday, though. And she'd settle into a new place. Start over again.

She walked into the kitchen. The cool granite was smooth under her fingers. Four walls, a few rooms, a view of the river— really, it was just an empty space. But it had been hers.

Her phone rang, and Max's name flashed onto the screen. This was it, the news she'd been waiting for.

"Max, the movers are heading your way. My place is completely empty."

"You're not going to like this, but you didn't get the apartment."

"What do you mean I didn't get the apartment? I signed the lease two days ago."

"One hour after someone else. They're refunding your deposit."

"Max, no, get me *that* apartment. The movers have that address." The movers. Cami ran out of the condo and down the stairs, looking for Clipboard Man.

"I found a place a little farther out. Three-bedroom town-home. New build, great community, but they want a year lease."

"Argh. Okay, well, if that's all that's available—"

"I'll keep looking, but let's decide by tomorrow."

Her condo was empty, her quaint apartment had fallen through, and a snitch was moving to Indy with her.

Cami retrieved Mama's painting, then took one final look at

her home. "Thanks for the memories." Then she closed and locked the door and stored the key in the Realtor's lockbox.

She closed her eyes, pressed her forehead against the cool wood door, and breathed. What was she going to do?

She grabbed her box and escaped to her car. She was staying with Annalise and Steve, but he was having a guys night and Annalise was finalizing details with Vicki.

"All right, Cami Jackson, you can go anywhere in the world you want to go. Where is it?"

She rested her forehead on the steering wheel. Hearts Bend. She'd go to the inn and convince Ben to stay in Tennessee and marry her.

She jerked upright. "No, no, no, girl. Scrub that thought now."

What she really needed to do was have it out with Dad. But did she have the energy? This was crazy. She had a night free and no place to go. Annalise was right. She needed a social life.

Firing up the Beemer, Cami stared at the garage wall, working up the nerve to drive across town and knock on Brant Jackson's door.

CHAPTER 16

*D*ad's swanky Green Hills townhome loomed in front of Cami. No wonder she didn't want a townhome—Dad's was always so unwelcoming. So un-homelike. Expensive but cold.

Cami parked her BMW in the driveway, drew a deep breath, and knocked on his front door—a solid black slab of wood. The sun was starting to dip below the horizon, and she welcomed the cool shade of the porch.

On the drive over, she'd realized this argument would be a continuation of the one they'd had in his office a few weeks ago.

Dad was still dressed in his work slacks and shirt, his collar open and a book in his hand. "Cami, what are you doing here?" He stepped aside for her to come in.

"You know why I'm here." She crossed his threshold and stood in his unadorned entryway. He'd moved here after Cami graduated from college and bought her own place. He'd divided all the furniture and dishes they'd had growing up between Annalise and Cami. As far as she knew, he'd taken nothing of their childhood home to this place. "Geoffrey Swanson? Really? You didn't even ask me."

"I don't have to ask you. He'll be a good second."

"Then you keep him. He'll be a good pain in my backside." Cami moved from the foyer to the living room. The entire place looked like a Peeps chick had upchucked its marshmallow center.

White walls, white floors. The only adornment was the unlit foyer chandelier and the one over the dining table, which was a whitewashed oak.

Mama had loved color, and Dad seemed to have washed every ounce of it out of his life and soul.

"Let's take this to my office." Dad headed for the room on the left and settled in the black leather desk chair behind his large cherry desk. Okay, he had some color in this bland place. The wall on the right was a floor-to-ceiling bookcase, but the rest of the walls were bare.

Cami took the seat across from Dad.

"I guess I should've talked to you about Geoffrey, but—"

"Yes, you should have. You ship me off without talking to me, then you hire my second-in-command without even so much as a by-your-leave. Dad, if you want Indy to succeed, you have to let me do my job." She stood, stretching as tall as she could above the desk. "I'm the future head of Akron, and you need to back up and stop treating me like a first-year intern."

She wanted to growl—no, roar, *Stop treating me like the fifteen-year-old who let Mama die!*

"You're right. I shouldn't have hired Geoffrey without consulting you."

"You shouldn't have hired him at all. I will hire my own staff. In fact..." She paused to consider her next words. "Geoff is fired. I'll hire my own second-in-command."

Dad regarded her with his steely expression. "Don't embarrass him. Keep it quiet. I'll find something else for him."

"Don't embarrass him? But you didn't mind embarrassing me by promoting him and sending the email."

"I didn't see it as embarrassing you, Cami."

"Well, it was humiliating. Would you have done that to Eric or William? Promote someone in their department, then send a company-wide email without telling them?"

"You've made your point." His tone set her back. Soft, contrite, almost repentant.

"Th-thank you." Cami eased back down to her chair. "But I have to ask, what's with the environmental survey of the inn, Dad? What are you up to? Ben was furious. He wants out of the deal. He claims I knew you'd pull a stunt like this, and if I didn't, I'm not strong enough to stop you. Everyone in Hearts Bend is afraid you'd demo the whole town if you had the chance."

"That's ridiculous. I blame Haley Danner. She painted me in a horrible light at the town council meeting even though Linus declared Akron was a friend to Hearts Bend."

"Then prove it. Fix the inn. Let's renovate. Were you really intending to tear it down? Were you going to talk to me about any of this? The inn is my acquisition, and I promised Ben I'd take care of it. Then you come rolling in with Dean's crew and—"

"Standard procedure, Cami. You know we do surveys on all of our properties, even if we don't pave the way for something new."

Well, if that didn't cool her jets a bit. "Right, well, still, I know you hate the inn."

"Did Ben tell you I stopped by as he was ranting about me and Akron?"

"He might have, but he was too busy canceling the contract."

"I don't hate the inn." Dad came around his desk and sat in the chair next to Cami. "It just has so many memories for me. Your mama and I used to go down to the inn all the time before the business took off. We'd dream and plan, then you girls came along, and we thought the inn was the perfect home away from home. We didn't have an ole family homestead, with both grandparents living out of state. Vern, Jean, and the inn provided that for us."

The tenderness in his voice raised her tears. For the first time in years, she was talking to her father. Her daddy. "Then I ruined everything. She died on my watch. And you hated me for it."

Dad angled forward and covered his face with his hands. "I hate myself for it, Cami. I got so busy with the business, putting my success above everything. When Mama died so suddenly, so young, I was angry and hurt. Angry at God. Your mama was a kind, loving, praying woman. Why did He take her? Why had I put her and you girls in second place? All I cared about was myself and my achievements. If I'd known—"

"But you said I let Mama die because I tried CPR before calling nine-one-one. If I'd called them first, she might have lived. You looked right at me and said it, Dad. 'You let your mother die.' Then you said you hoped Annalise was around if anything ever happened to you."

The great and powerful Brant Jackson dropped to his knees, sobbing softly, his hand on Cami's knee. "Forgive me, Cami, please." His shoulders shook as the sobs took over.

"Oh, Dad—" She slid out of the chair and knelt next to him. He held her as they wept, washing away the last fifteen years. "I forgive you, I forgive you."

As quickly as the tearful repentance had begun, it ended.

Dad rose up and stepped away, dealing with the residue of his tears.

Cami yanked several tissues from the box on the bookshelf.

"I've been wanting to talk to you for years," Dad said. "But you were so angry at me when you were a teen, and I thought bringing it up would only make you angrier. Plus, every speech I rehearsed in my head just sounded like I was defending myself. Annalise assured me you knew I'd only lashed out from grief. That I didn't mean it. But, Cami, I should've manned up and asked your forgiveness." Dad returned to the chair by Cami. "I'm sorry. Truly."

She wiped the tears from her eyes and smiled at him. "I came over here to bawl you out and, look, I get repentance and healing. Who knew?"

"Your mother would say the Lord knew."

Cami laughed and reached for another tissue. "Yes, she would. She'd be upset we stopped going to church and exercising our faith."

"I've started going back." Dad looked so cute, like a little boy admitting his parents were right. "Doug Reynolds reached out, asked me to a men's meeting, and the moment I walked in, I sensed God's presence. I figure if He could make Himself known to me after all my years in the wilderness, I should give Him a second chance."

Cami answered with a soft, sweet sob. "Mama would be so happy. I've been giving God a second thought as well."

"So you and I are good?" Dad said.

She nodded, then leaned on her father's shoulder. "I love you."

"I love you too, Cami-girl. Let's do better going forward."

"Absolutely." She sat back, brushing away more tears. "We're going to be the best papa and auntie for Annalise's baby."

"Yes, we are." Dad gave Cami a fist bump. "When she told me she was pregnant, I knew I had to humble up and make things right between us. I don't want offense and judgment in our family. I want us to love one another, be there for each other."

"Does this mean you'll finally let me decorate this place? Dad, come on, nothing but white with a touch of black? How can you stand it?"

Dad laughed. "Okay, okay, fine, you can decorate, but I have a picture I'd like you to use."

He walked to the front closet and opened the door, pulling out a familiar painting: her red camellia.

"H-how did you get this?"

"Ben was kind enough to let me have it. And if you're going to decorate, I'd like this front and center. Just keep things simple and tasteful."

"Those words are my middle names." Cami touched his hand. "Do you want the painting Mama hung in the inn lobby too? She painted it for you."

"No, my girl, she painted it for you."

Ben picked up the contract from Frank Hardy and flipped through it one more time. He'd upped the offer to five hundred thousand. Probably because Mr. Graham guilted him into it, but the property was worth so much more.

Keith had called with some prospective buyers, but so far, no progress. Ben had reached out to the Grangers in Georgia, but they'd just purchased a similar project in Johnson City and decided to pass. They wished Ben luck, but what he needed was a miracle.

Tomorrow was August fifteenth, and he had to get back to

Sydney. He felt a twinge of regret that he'd miss the wedding. On the surface, the inn looked good—though there was still work to be done. But the cottages had been painted and furnished, and the grounds had been trimmed and manicured to perfection.

Insurance would cover the kitchen upgrade, but Ben had paid the deposit to get things going. Walt, along with the contractor, had gutted it yesterday. Annalise had found a caterer who was willing to work without access to the kitchen.

With his experience and contacts in the industry, Ben had gotten a great deal on an industrial oven, dishwasher, and fridge. Frank was getting more than his money's worth.

But was it all for nothing? What if Frank leveled the place the minute Ben left town? He'd indicated to Mr. Graham he wanted to keep the inn as a town landmark, but something about this deal felt off to Ben.

Maybe he should humble up and call Cami. The idea made him cringe. He'd leveled her on the phone, hadn't listened to a word she'd said. Just blamed and accused her. By the twist in his spirit, he knew he needed to apologize no matter what happened with the inn.

Ben glanced around the old office, which was starting to feel so comfortable. He'd prayed two weeks straight sitting at this desk. While he wasn't a holy roller, declaring the Gospel from the rooftop, he was confident he'd spend the rest of his life pursuing the God of love.

His gaze fell on the picture of Granny and Granddaddy he'd knocked off two months ago. He felt their happiness, their joy and hope for all life had in store for them.

"Y'all are face-to-face with Jesus. Tell Him I need a clear answer here. Do I sign Frank's contract or hold out for an eleventh hour surprise?"

He closed his eyes and breathed in, trying to be still and

listen. Then with a wash of peace, he grabbed a pen and put it on the signature line.

"Here goes." He was just about to sign when—

"Hey, Ben!" Myrtle May hollered from the front desk.

"On my way." Ben dropped the pen and headed for the lobby, where he found Myrtle May holding one of the old doorknobs.

"Closet knob from Room Ten," she said. "Just when we have a big fancy wedding on our heels."

Ben reached for the antique piece. "I don't think we have any more like this. We'll have to try to find something online that looks similar."

"Ask Ray. He'll know."

"I know from the last doorknob that fell off. The one I found was the last in the box."

Myrtle May just stared. The one that said *Look again.*

Out in the barn, Ben had begun searching for the knob box when he heard Ray call out. "Ben? Back here."

"Myrtle May sent me out to look for doorknobs."

"I just set the knob can on the workbench."

"How convenient." Ben walked around the shelves to the workbench. Sure enough, the can was on the bench next to a blueprint tube.

"Ray, what's in the tube?" Ben glanced in the can to find a single doorknob. "Are you kidding me with these doorknobs? Is this the can of endless doorknobs?"

"Got me. I think the Good Lord is saying He's the one that opens and closes doors."

"I wish He'd make it clear which doors I'm to open and close."

Ben opened the canister and rolled out the blueprints to see an expansion plan for the inn. More cottages, a bigger pool, even a lazy river, and a small café area to expand into a full-service restaurant. He hadn't known his grandparents had had this much ambition about the place.

But plans like this would bring the inn into the modern era and make it extremely competitive. Keeping it quaint and homey, the place would be a destination for weddings, receptions, parties, and reunions.

Except expansion took cash. Which he did not have. And he was probably selling. Stan from the bank had suggested Ben look for an investor, but that took a ton of time and work. Which made the two lost weeks he hadn't known Cami wasn't buying the inn all the more critical.

Ben held up the knob and grinned. One knob. Because one knob was all he needed. Was this a sign?

If he stayed at the inn, God *would* meet his needs. It might not be the prestigious career of working for VJR. He'd not make near the same money, but he'd be contributing to the community, one where practically everyone knew his name. He'd be the one to make a place of rest and refuge for those in need. He'd touch hearts in a way he could never do managing a corporate resort.

Without even thinking, he began composing a letter to Jim.

...regret to inform you...official resignation. Jordan...as my replacement...knows as much as I do.

He, Ben Carter, was coming home. All the way home. To Hearts Bend Inn.

"Ta-da!"

Ben jerked at the sound of Ray's voice. If he didn't know better, he'd believe the man was reading his mind.

"Ray? What's up?"

The gardener appeared from between a second bank of shelves with a big smile and the old wrought iron and wood bench.

CHAPTER 17

The moment Cami had left Dad's town house the other night, she'd known her life had changed. She felt lighter, brighter. And the urge to paint and create was stronger than ever.

Ben had been on her mind. A lot. She'd start to text him, then chicken out every time. She had to somehow transfer her confidence in closing a property deal to her love life. To her love for Ben.

While she'd gained so much healing after Dad had asked her forgiveness, she still couldn't see a way to reach out to Ben.

Besides, weren't they headed on very different paths? Why start something they couldn't finish? She'd decided to at least tell him the environmental study was a standard Akron deal and the company had no intention of destroying the inn.

She'd removed his contract from the project board with a bit of sadness and tried to move forward. There were plenty of things to distract her between Vicki's wedding and the move to Indy.

Then Dad had called her into his office with the most surprising offer.

"I was thinking you could stay here, become the director of operations with a plan to make vice president in two years. What do you think? I'll send Geoffrey to Indianapolis. I spoke with Astrid, and she still wants to go. She's apparently met someone there."

"What? That rat, she never said."

Dad grabbed her hand. *"I want you here with me and your sister and your new niece or nephew."*

"Niece."

"I'll miss you too much if I send you to Indy. Even when I first assigned you, I almost regretted it, but—"

"Yes, Dad, yes. I'll stay. I never wanted to move. I don't even have a place to live up there. Everything kept falling through. I want to be here for Annalise, the baby, and you." She squeezed his hand. *"But if we're really being honest, I don't want to be director or vice president. I love buying and selling, I love working for you. But, Dad, I want time to breathe, relax, paint. I want to bring back the part of me that was Mama. I was so busy trying for your approval, I left her behind."*

Dad had held her so tight she'd thought he'd never let go. And that was fine with her.

So, she wasn't moving after all. She'd heard Annalise's scream all the way across town when they'd called to tell her. Even though she was busy with the wedding, she'd shared in Cami's excitement in the change of events.

However, the good news had dumped her into the deep end, requiring her to bring Geoffrey up to speed on everything and find a new Nashville place to live. If she'd had any doubts about her decision, they'd ended the moment Marta called— one hour after Cami had put her on the hunt for a new place.

You're not going to believe it, but I found the most charming and perfect bungalow not five minutes from your sister.

Cami had signed the lease that afternoon and called the movers to haul her stuff back to Nashville. They were willing to store her belongings for a few weeks. The place needed work, but the owner had said she could do what she wanted as long as it didn't involve any demo.

Once she'd settled in and handed the reins of Indy to Geoff, she could no longer avoid the obvious. She had to talk to Ben. He'd be leaving on Wednesday, if not sooner. What if he'd already left?

A quick text to her sister told her he was still in town. In fact, he was staying through the wedding.

"Really? Doesn't he need to be in Sydney?"

"Apparently, he's extended his stay. He found a new buyer for the inn."

A new buyer? Well, what had she expected? And for the life of her, she couldn't think why she hadn't offered to buy it again once Dad had pledged to not tear it down.

Because she loved him. Because she didn't want him to tell her no again.

But here she was, Wednesday before the wedding, heading to Hearts Bend because Annalise had sent an *all hands on deck* message and Cami had replied with a *Yes, ma'am.*

She took the day off and prayed all the way down I-65. As she eased up the inn's long driveway, the gravel popped under her tires. She parked in the shade next to Annalise's Volkswagen and headed off to find her sister, pausing when she passed an electrician's truck.

What was going on? A delivery truck drove past her and parked by the kitchen door.

From inside, Myrtle May could be heard directing traffic.

"Over there, Ted. Careful now, don't scratch the hardwoods. We just had them polished."

Making her way around to the front door with a floral wreath hung in the center, Cami found Annalise at the front desk, iPad in hand, going over something with Ben. They stood under Mama's painting.

Cami hung back, waiting for them to finish, and gazed at the image on the wall. *She painted it for you,* Dad had said.

But when she'd asked why, he'd simply said, *In due time.*

She took in the pastoral scene with green trees and a field flooded with golden light. Then the couple on the bench.

Can we jump into the painting? Ben had once asked.

If only they could. Cami shifted her gaze to him. Dressed in his usual jeans and T-shirt, hat with the bill in back, he was tan, relaxed, and smiling. He'd been gorgeous before, but in this moment, he was heart stopping.

"Finally!" Annalise gave Cami a quick hug. "What took you so long?"

"You only texted two hours ago."

Annalise's phone rang and she stepped away. "Caterer," she whispered. "Nicole, give me good news."

Ben smiled. "She's really been scrambling since the kitchen is torn apart. I think we can get the refrigerator up and running in time for the wedding, and Tina over at Ella's volunteered her ovens if we needed. But Vicki had to invite her to the wedding." Ben stepped a little closer. "How've you been? How's Indy?"

"I'm not going. Gave the project to someone else. Dad and I had the heart-to-heart we've needed to have for fifteen years, and neither one of us wanted me to go. What about you? Aren't you needed in Sydney?"

"I resigned."

"What? Ben, why?"

"If I told you it was the miracle of antique doorknobs in a tin bucket, would you believe me?"

Cami laughed. "Oddly enough, yes."

"Look, Cami, I'm so sorry about that phone call." When he reached for her hand, her heart gave a happy thump against her chest. "I realized I had some resentment toward my folks for dropping me off here and never coming back for me even though they said they would. When I saw the environmental surveyors and they said they were prepping to tear this place down, I thought you'd broken your promise to me."

"It's SOP with Akron. We do surveys with every property. I'm sorry I didn't tell you."

"But I blamed you, and that's what your dad did to you when your mom died."

"Goodness," she said, brushing away tears. "I feel like a leaky faucet these days." She raised her gaze to his. "I'm sorry about Dean, and really, for the last week of silence. I should've called."

"No, *I* should've called. I flew off the handle, said things that were uncalled for. I'm sorry."

"Me too." She didn't resist when he pulled her into a hug. In his arms, her world was right again.

When he released her, he said, "I have a surprise. Come on."

He led her outside and down the garden path. When his hand brushed hers, the excitement and tingles from the Fourth of July returned.

"Where are we—"

They rounded the path, and there, under the oak tree, sat the bench.

The bench.

"You found it."

189

"Ray did, yes. He fixed it up and brought it out here this morning."

"It's just like the painting. You know she and Daddy always sat here."

"Yeah, he told me when he came to the inn."

"I still can't believe he didn't tell me he was here. What else did he say?" Cami perched on the edge of the seat, then slid back. Perfect.

"He said the couple in the painting was not them."

"Not Mama and Dad?"

"He said your mom had a dream about coming to visit here in their later years. They were coming to visit us. We're the couple in the painting, Cami."

"She painted you and me? W-what? I don't understand. What dream?"

"She dreamed we married, but she didn't want to force fate. Your dad said she wanted the Lord to be our matchmaker." Ben joined her on the bench, taking her hand in his. "I still love you."

Cami brushed her hand over his soft beard and gently kissed Ben's lips. "I still love you."

How long they lingered on the bench—their bench— enjoying sweet kisses and whispered words of love, making promises and plans, Cami couldn't tell. But the afternoon was bliss. Pure, unadulterated bliss.

Ben's first event—the wedding—went off without a hitch. The eighty-two guests raved about the inn, and several of them talked to Ben about future bookings. Two anniversaries and a couple of birthday parties. And one possible wedding.

The catering was flawless as the team moved between the inn's refrigerator and Tina's kitchen.

The tent and wooden chairs, the arch and flowers, the string quartet were magical. Vicki was a stunning bride, and when her groom teared up as she came down the aisle, Ben felt it in his chest.

At the reception, some of Vicki's band members filled their corner of Hearts Bend with music. Buck Mathews and his wife, JoJo, attended, and toward the end of the night, he and Vicki surprised the guests with a new song they'd written and recorded together.

But for Ben, the best part of the night was Cami. She was beautiful. Light and free. She'd taken the week off from work and all but lived at the inn. She'd set up Cottage Three for Vicki and her bridesmaids. The small floral arrangements, snacks, and mirrors Cami had arranged made the room shine. Without Cami's mindful attention to the cottage, it wouldn't have been half so special. Vicki cried when she saw Cami's thoughtfulness and care.

"So Cottage Three?" Ben said, holding her close. "No longer a place of pain?"

She shook her head and kissed him. "A place of love."

Annalise found him and said the few wedding photos Vicki's assistant had posted on social media were getting all sorts of inquiries about the location.

"I'm getting married next March. Is this place available?" a petite woman had asked as she snuggled into a lanky, dark-hair man.

"Vicki just put you on the map," Annalise said.

The band started the melody to "I Will Always Love You," and Ben led Cami to the dance floor.

"I've been thinking," she said. "You're going to need investors for this place."

"You're right, but I think I need to be very particular. Can't get into business with just anyone."

"True, true," Cami said, peering into his eyes. "She needs to be smart and savvy, with business experience."

"Agreed, but where do I find such an amazing woman?"

She laughed, then kissed him. "I want to invest. I have money from the sale of my condo, and besides buying ridiculously expensive shoes, I put most of my bonuses in savings."

"Your dad offered to invest too."

"You're kidding."

"He said it's what Macie would want. He said he owed you anyway for all the pain he left you in."

"He didn't really leave me in pain, and I don't own the inn. How is investing—"

"It would if you'd consider a future with me."

Cami shifted her gaze to take in the crowd around them on the dance floor. "Ben Carter, you're not asking me to marry you, are you?"

"Not right now. You'll known when I'm asking." He turned her toward him in time with the music. "But I am asking if you'd consider working toward making your mama's painting a reality."

Her eyes welled up and a sassy grin spread across her face. "I'd consider it."

Oh, what a glorious kiss followed. He lifted her off the ground, swung her around, then kissed her again.

He didn't need fancy resorts or to live in cities like Sydney or Hong Kong to have adventure. All he needed was a purpose and the woman he loved.

In truth, his adventures were just beginning.

CHAPTER 18

*C*ami deemed today the perfect day. The cool October breeze moderated the heat of the afternoon sun, and the blue sky was just the right shade.

In a twist that had surprised them all, Walt and Myrtle May had eloped after Vicki's wedding and had just returned from their honeymoon to set up house in the owner's cottage. Walt was happy to leave his bachelor pad behind and move in with Myrtle May, though Cami suspected he snuck off to his old fishing shack whenever he could.

But they were happy. She saw love in their eyes.

As she set up her easel and chair, her engagement ring caught the light and scattered a prism of color across the canvas. Ben had proposed with the ring a few weeks after Vicki's wedding. Took Cami out to the bench, got down on one knee, and slid a simple but beautiful diamond onto her finger.

She and Annalise were busy planning a March wedding, getting as much work done before the arrival of baby Macie Camellia in February.

Vicki's wedding had exploded Annalise's business so much

Annalise had hired two assistants. The inn's business had also increased, the rooms and cottages at eighty percent capacity. Ben was working on organizing all the scheduled events, which fit right into all of his corporate experience.

With her and Dad's investment money, they paid off the loan and continued upgrades on the inn. Ben had taken the old plans to an architect for modifications, at the very least bringing the structures and elements up to the twenty-first century.

Cami split her time between Hearts Bend and Nashville, living in Cottage Three Friday night through Sunday night. Even though she'd backed off Akron duties, she'd been killing it with acquisitions and had recently landed two of the largest deals in Akron history.

Guess that was what she got for letting the Lord lead her life. Not that every day was easy. She and Ben had weathered their first few fights, learning each other's ways.

In late September, Dad had had a small heart episode, so the doc had him eating more "mush," according to Dad, but he admittedly felt better. That had been a bit of a scare for them all.

Geoffrey had called at the end of September begging for Cami to come up and help with one of his projects. She'd spent a week with Astrid, who'd finally, finally found a good man.

But for God...

The family had started their first monthly gathering in October. Dad, Annalise, and Steve had come to the inn, and Ben had barbecued. They'd played cornhole and laughed until their sides hurt.

But for God...

The best part, besides Ben's love and kisses—Cami was painting again, which was why she'd come out to this spot.

Today was the day to finish Mama's painting. She planned to give it to Dad for Christmas. He'd painted the walls of his place a soft gray and added a blue paint to one of the living room walls. Slowly but surely, color was coming back to Dad's life. Cami's red camellia took center stage in his living room. Dad had insisted that she decorate around her picture.

"There you are." Ben walked toward her, the breeze pressing his T-shirt against his taut middle. "I'm starved. Angelo's?"

Cami looked at her paint brushes and the basket of her acrylics. "I'd love to."

Maybe Dad should've taken more time to be with Mama and his girls, but Mama had borne some responsibility. Dad had felt she'd loved her work more than him.

Painting could wait. Growing in love with Ben trumped everything.

"Keith called. He found a house in town that has our name written all over it," Ben said, taking her hand as they walked toward the inn's old truck. "A craftsman. Want to swing by, take a look?"

Love, peace, finishing Mama's painting, heading off to pizza with the love of her life before touring their possible dream house... What more could a girl want?

Nothing, absolutely nothing.

SNICKERDOODLES RECIPE

Want to make the cookie that inspired Walt's snickerdoodles?
Bon appétit!

INGREDIENTS:
   1/2 cup (1 stick) room temperature, unsalted butter
   1-1/2 cups all-purpose flour
   1 cup sugar
   1 egg
   1/2 tsp vanilla
   1/4 tsp baking baking soda
   1/4 tsp cream of tartar

TO ROLL BEFORE BAKING:
   2 TB sugar
   1 tsp ground cinnamon

INSTRUCTIONS:

   1. Preheat oven to 375°.

2. In a stand mixer (or use electric hand mixer), beat butter on medium to high speed for 30 seconds.

3. Add to butter: half of the flour, sugar, egg, vanilla, baking soda and cream of tartar.

4. Beat until mixed.

5. Add in rest of flour and beat until completely combined.

6. Cover and let chill for at least one hour.

7. Combine the 2 TB of sugar and 1 tsp of cinnamon well.

8. Roll the dough into 1-inch balls.

9. Roll each ball in the sugar/cinnamon mixture.

10. Place cookies on an uncreased cookie sheet 2 inches apart.

11. Bake for 10-11 minutes, watching for edges of cookies to be golden.

12. Remove and let stand about 2 minutes, then move to wire racks to cool.

Recipe adapted with permission from Tammy Karasek

CONNECT WITH SUNRISE

Thank you so much for reading *You'll Be Mine*. We hope you enjoyed the story. If you did, would you be willing to do us a favor and leave a review? It doesn't have to be long—just a few words to help other readers know what they're getting. (But no spoilers! We don't want to wreck the fun!) Thank you again for reading!

We'd love to hear from you—not only about this story, but about any characters or stories you'd like to read in the future. Contact us at www.sunrisepublishing.com/contact.

We also have a monthly update that contains sneak peeks, reviews, upcoming releases, and fun stuff for our reader friends. Sign up at www.sunrisepublishing.com.

OTHER HEARTS BEND NOVELS

Hearts Bend Collection

One Fine Day

You'll Be Mine

Hearts Bend Novels by Rachel Hauck

The Wedding Chapel

The Wedding Shop

The Wedding Dress Christmas

To Save a King

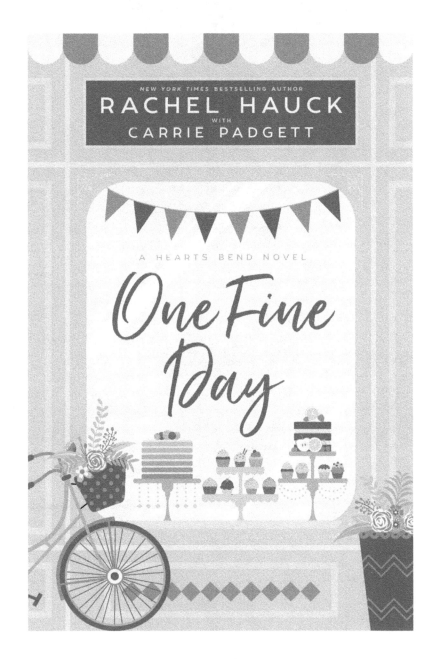

Turn the page for a sneak peek of *One Fine Day*, Book 1 in the Hearts Bend Collection ...

SNEAK PEEK

ONE FINE DAY

Of all the things Chloe LaRue had ever dreamed she'd be doing on a fine Monday afternoon in February, folding laundry in her old bedroom wasn't one of them.

Married to a handsome athlete of some kind? Maybe. Living in Paris? Oh, she'd hoped so. Making a name for herself as a pastry chef, maybe even owning her own café? Definitely.

She'd achieved most of these things, her dreams, until life kicked her to the curb.

Baking petit fours during the day and dancing in clubs with her gorgeous, extreme sports competitor husband all night, sure.

But thirty and widowed and moving back home to take care of her mother? Never saw that one coming.

She dropped the laundry basket on her bed and looked around. Mom hadn't changed much in here, other than replacing the ratty old carpet. The walls were still a loud purple, the bookcase stuffed with her old journals, and the Jimmy Eat World poster with curling and brown edges remained taped to the closet door.

Whoever said starting over, having a clean slate, was a good thing? Probably the same wise guy who said time heals all wounds. Because neither seemed to be happening for her.

She slid open the closet door and laughed softly. There were her Doc Martens, still on the floor in the exact spot she'd left them after graduating from Rock Mill High. Her studded belts still hung from the closet hooks, and her black emo clothes remained on the hangers.

If only she could go back and tell that lonely, angst-filled teenager to lighten up, to give herself—and others—a little grace. That girl who'd wanted to be different yet the same as everyone else had found herself in culinary school, and it was the best of both worlds. Her emo roots—the only Fall Out Boy fan in a school of Carrie Underwood wannabes—had given her the strength and fortitude for life in a fast-paced, high-pressure kitchen. For life as a pastry chef.

Chloe pulled a black hoodie off the hanger to make room for her red wool coat.

Oh Mom, you've changed so few things since I left. But why would she? Mom had lost so much. Chloe didn't blame her for hanging onto precious things. Like preserving her daughter's room. Chloe never dreamed she'd lose a second man she loved. That she'd end up widowed, just like Mom.

A week ago, she'd been spinning hot caramel into birds' nests to adorn cakes as the pastry chef at Bistro Gaspard, a small but highly regarded restaurant in the Bastille district of Paris. Then Mom called. *"So...I have a little bit of cancer."* Chloe had dropped everything and returned to sleepy, slow, country-touristy Hearts Bend, Tennessee.

She'd lost her father when she was eight. Then her husband ten months ago, when she was twenty-nine. She flat refused to lose her mother. She'd will her to live, or—cue the irony and cliché—die trying.

A meow rustled the silence of the room and Chloe turned to see Honey, Mom's ginger cat, curled up on the bed. She stared at Chloe as if she understood her thoughts and spoke up to keep her from tumbling down into the familiar dark hole of pity and sadness.

"I'm working on it, Honey. I promise."

Honey narrowed her hazel-green eyes, waited a second, then seemingly satisfied, stretched and tucked her head into the crook of a leg.

A bit of light broke through the February clouds and leaked into the room, dripping over the window seat where Chloe used to read and dream about a life beyond her tiny hometown. Marriage. A pastry career. Maybe even her own café or bistro someday. She smiled, breathing easy, feeling free, at least for now, of the burdens she'd brought with her from France. The bare branches of the tree outside her second-story bedroom window allowed dim sunshine to puddle on the newly installed beige carpet.

But she didn't have time for pondering or the heart for any more painful memories, so she tipped over the laundry basket and settled down to folding as the sun retreated behind the clouds again. She snapped a cotton T-shirt and smoothed out the wrinkles. Coming home to help Mom didn't mean she was *moving* backward, right? Coming home allowed her to regroup, pass Go, collect her two hundred dollars, and—in a few months—get back in the pastry chef game.

Coming home meant she was looking *forward*.

Her earlier life, with its hopes and dreams, had ended so suddenly. She and Jean-Marc had talked of purchasing a café, had that odd, pointless argument about money, then she had found herself suddenly swallowed up by the dark pain of a graveside goodbye. The confusion of their emptied bank account and papers shoved at her to sign only solidified her feelings of loss and despair. The papers that her in-laws assured her were formalities needed to settle Jean-Marc's shares of the family business. When the whirlwind had settled, she'd faced the abrupt starkness of empty days without the man she loved.

Oh Jean-Marc, I'm sorry...so, so sorry.

Within weeks, the joy of blending flour, sugar, and butter into macarons, croissants, and èclairs had become a weight. Simple things like piping icing on a petit four became a laborious task. She battled a thick mental fog, and nothing seemed to nurse her broken heart. Getting out of bed felt like a chore. Chloe paced all night and slept all day, calling in sick to work often. Even when the sun was shining, her grief made it seem as though the whole world was cloudy. She thought she was going crazy. Often, she felt as though she was dying as well.

A colleague had recommended a grief support group, which she reluctantly joined. The leader assured her all she felt was normal. But if this was *normal*, she wanted out. What was the point of living when all her dreams—a café of their own and a cottage in the French countryside—were buried six feet in the ground with her husband?

Her breaking point had come last month, when she found herself lying on the couch of her cold apartment, calling Jean-Marc's phone just to hear his voicemail greeting. She would end up weeping and inhaling a faint trace of his scent in the threads of the old quilt. Then she'd remembered the good times, how he'd finally believed in her dream to own a café in Deux Jardins—and the grief started all over again.

When Mom called, it was as if life, fate, or perhaps God had taken pity on her and delivered her from the tomb of *Life and Love Lost*. Breast cancer, Mom said, trying to sound chipper. Chloe couldn't pack fast enough. She'd loaded suitcases and boxes with her rolling pins and cake pans, dishes, photos, one ridiculously expensive men's watch, clothes, and mementos of the life she'd built with Jean-Marc. She found herself buying a one-way ticket home.

Okay, Chloe, enough. No more dwelling on the past. Look to the future. However bleak and barren it may be.

For the next few minutes, she set up house in her old room, layering her old dresser drawers with her clean shirts, jeans and shorts, socks and undies, hanging up her coats and dresses—the remnants of her Paris life an odd juxtaposition to the girl she'd once been.

"Honey..." She held the laundry basket in her hand and smiled at the cat. "I'm leaving now. Keep my bed warm, okay?" Hand on the light switch, she was about to turn off the lamp when a glint of sunshine burst through the trees, bounced off the dresser mirror, and illuminated the row of pictures tucked into the mirror's edge. Chloe set the basket in the hallway, then crossed the room and leaned in for a closer look at the official photo of her high school cast and crew of *The Importance of Being Earnest.* Oh boy, that had been a fun production. She'd been in her "I'm a unique emo girl" element as a stagehand for the high school play, working behind the scenes, pulling the curtains, adjusting props.

JoJo Castle—Mathews, now—had played Gwendolen Fairfax. JoJo always won the female leads, but she had the talent and was always sweet to the crew, never stuck-up or snobby. Would she still be the same since she'd married Buck Mathews, the biggest artist in country music? Chloe imagined she'd find out since Buck and JoJo lived in Hearts Bend when he wasn't on tour. They were bound to run into each other in the town square.

Chloe replaced the picture in the mirror's brown, wooden frame and pulled out the next one—a photobooth strip taken at the fair that summer before their senior year. She and Sam Hardy made faces at the camera and each other. Sam...with his dark hair and deep brown eyes. Did he still have the stubborn curl that fell on his forehead? He'd done well, *really* well, as a first-round draft pick from University of Tennessee to the Titans. He'd been their franchise quarterback ever since.

Oooh, I had such a crush on you back in the day, Sammy.

She reached for the framed photo of Daddy on the dresser. How she'd love to feel his arms around her in one of his bear hugs, to bake his favorite pound cake for him one more time, to talk to him about Jean-Marc. She may have only known him for eight years, but Daddy had always made things better. He was her hero.

I miss you so much, Daddy. She ran a finger over the image of his hair, which was a tad too long for a hustling businessman, but he loved his ole '70s style. She smiled and tsked.

Now you're forever shaggy, Daddy.

A soft knock sounded at the door and Mom poked her head in. "Can I help with anything?" Her gaze drifted to Daddy's photo. "You remember when that was taken? At his last company picnic." She didn't speak the obvious. *A few weeks before he was killed.* "Twenty-two years and I still miss him."

Mom came the rest of the way into the room and picked up a different photo. One of Chloe and Jean-Marc at their wedding, coming down the aisle after the minister pronounced them husband and wife, their arms raised in victory. "I didn't know I'd left this here," Mom said softly. "I'll take it—"

"Mom, it's okay." Chloe set the gilded frame back on the dresser. She liked her expression in the photo. Would she ever smile that proudly, that excitedly again? "It's been almost a year since he died. I can see our picture without falling apart." But only recently. "Besides, I look really good here."

Mom laughed and after a second, Chloe joined her. Also only recently, she'd started to laugh again. Which seemed a sort of consolation prize for leaving Paris: her job, her memories, even her in-laws, whom she loved.

Being in Hearts Bend gave her a little window on life. Some semblance of home. Maybe she'd find the freedom to dream again.

"I have more photos with my things." Chloe glanced around the room toward her boxes, spied the one she wanted, and pulled out her favorite wedding photo, an image of her and Jean-Marc with their parents. "You looked beautiful, *Maman*, in your vintage Dior dress. Vivienne and Albert"—she gave the soft French pronunciation, Al-bare—"were so gracious and welcoming to us."

The five of them stood outside the old stone church near the LaRue family villa in Provence. Lavender fields behind them shimmered in the sun. In this photograph, Chloe smiled up at Jean-Marc while he gazed down at her with a tender expression. She remembered how his eyes had shone with love. They had been happy, so happy that day.

So how did it all end in a sudden death after a massive argument? There were moments when she couldn't really remember who had started the debate, or why. It had just seemed to snowball like an avalanche...

Chloe winced, a cold heartache pricking her moment of peace, and set the picture back in the box.

"Can we set this one out?" Mom retrieved it. "I think it will help you to grieve and recover if you remember the good times, darling."

"Y-yeah, sure." Mom knew some of the story of how Jean-Marc had died. But not all of it. Chloe peered in the box and, seeing Jean-Marc's watch, reached for it. This wretched thing had caused their first big fight, a few months after the wedding. She'd been furious when he told her what he'd paid for it.

"Why? You don't need it. A watch meant for scuba diving

with what, a chronograph and chronometer? You're a rock climber, Jean-Marc, a skier, not a scuba diver."

"Not yet, no. But I will be, chère cœur. Soon."

What a silly thing to fight about. If he wanted the watch so he could learn to scuba dive safely, he should have it. It was for his *safety*, after all. She set the watch on her dresser next to the photo. *Their* photo. Husband and wife. The couple who had stood in the chapel and pledged their love for as long as they lived.

An image flashed across her mind from Jean-Marc's graveside service—which happened every time she wandered any distance down memory lane. A blonde woman speaking with her in-laws in hushed tones and how they'd quieted and glanced at one another dubiously when Chloe approached. But she'd caught the whispered "*affaire de cœur*" hanging in the air.

Affair of the heart.

"Chloe? Are you all right?" Mom roped her arm around Chloe's shoulder. "Are you glad to be home? Truly?"

"Yeah, um, I'm fine." Mom had been there that day as well, but she'd seen and heard nothing. If she had, she would've asked. That was Mom's way. "I'm truly glad to be home. I couldn't let you go through cancer treatment on your own. I'm where I need to be."

Mom's eyes glistened as she looked away. For her, Chloe knew, talking about the next months and year only made her diagnosis all too real. Too threatening.

"Did you see the rest of the pictures on the mirror?" Mom said, leaning in, hands clasped behind her back. "I've only dusted around them for the past decade." Mom motioned to the strip of Chloe and Sam. "I remember that summer. You and Sam spent hours in the Hardys' pool while I was learning his father's business, training to be his admin." Mom had been working for Frank Hardy, Sam's dad, ever since.

"Does Sam still call his dad Frank?" Until Chloe had seen the old stage crew picture and the photo strip, she'd not thought of her teenage friends in ages. Except Sam. Jean-Marc was a fan of American football and enjoyed telling his football-loving friends *his* wife had attended high school with the great Sam Hardy. Jean-Marc kept up with Sam via sports websites as well as the good ole *Hearts Bend Tribune*, which bragged about their hometown boy every chance they got. Jean-Marc recited details about Sam's successes, and they'd talked of a trip home last summer to see Mom, explore Chloe's childhood haunts, and of course, arrange an introduction to Sam.

"As far as I know he still does," Mom said. "Sam rarely comes home. Frank mentions him once in a while, but I'm sure he misses him, even if he's too proud to admit it."

"Sounds like they're both stubborn."

"In a word, yes." Mom laughed as she turned to peek into one of Chloe's boxes lined up along the wall. "Try working for one of them. Ooo, your teddy bear." Mom reached in for the trusty old stuffed animal, the one Chloe had moved halfway around the world—*twice.*

"For your bed," Mom said, her eyes glistening again.

She'd had the bear made from Dad's favorite flannel shirt, and Chloe liked to imagine his fragrance still resided in the threads. Maybe she'd have another made from Jean-Marc's dark blue thermal. Keep them both on her bed, make it a memorial. She shook her head, throwing off depressing thoughts.

"It's about dinner time," Mom said. "Are you hungry? We could run to Ella's Diner. Tina

reinstated Monday night pie nights. If we go early, we can get a booth by the front window."

Chloe sighed and sat on the edge of the bed, a fresh batch of tears rising.

Mom placed a hand on Chloe's arm. "What is it, darling?"

She flopped backward onto the old soft quilt. "Just this... life. I don't mind being here, I want to be here, honest. But I can't get it out of my head entirely that this is not what I planned on doing when I was turning thirty. I've been a mess since Jean-Marc died. One minute I'm angry at him. The next, weeping and sobbing and missing him so much, it physically pains my chest. I feel like I'm having a heart attack."

Mom lay down next to her and Chloe rested her head on Mom's shoulder. "You know what I'm going to say, don't you?"

Chloe sat up. "Yes, so don't." She wasn't ready to hear —again—that she'd get over losing her husband, she'd go on with life, maybe even find a new love. Yada, yada. *Whatever.* Clearly Mom didn't practice what she preached. Twenty-two years after Daddy died, she was still alone.

Alone. Which was another reason why Chloe had left Paris to come home and help Maman.

"Why don't we bake tomorrow? That always cheered you up as a girl."

Chloe's eyes filled with tears. "MeMaw's vanilla cake?"

Mom kissed her forehead. "That's the one. Unless you've come up with some fancy French pastry that cures your blues."

"No way. MeMaw's cake is the *only* thing to soothe a sad soul."

"So, dinner?" Mom elbowed Chloe's side. "Ella's?"

Chloe surveyed the boxes stacked under the window seat— the ones she'd shipped at an exorbitant fee from France—and considered more unpacking. But where would she put the dishes or linens she'd acquired in her life as an ex-pat? The remnants of nearly eight years with Jean-Marc. She was here for now but not staying forever. This was just to get herself together and to see Mom through chemo and radiation.

Chloe drew a breath with a side glance at Mom. Now was as good a time as ever. "We've talked about Dad's death, Jean-

Marc, my return home, dinner, and vanilla cake, but not why I'm really here."

Mom got up and moved to the window. "You know why. I feel like if I talk about it, I'm feeding it. If I ignore it, maybe it will go away." She looked at Chloe. "Silly, I know."

"Not silly. I understand." Chloe slipped off the bed. "What time is your appointment in the morning?" The what-to-expect-during-treatment appointment would be Chloe's first opportunity to introduce herself to Mom's medical team. Chemo would start officially the next day.

"Nine o'clock. I hope you don't regret coming home from Paris to chauffeur me to the doctor or chemo clinic. I'm glad you're home, don't get me wrong, I just wish it wasn't to take care of me. What about your career?"

"You are more important than my career. At least death has taught me one good lesson. Besides, I wasn't in the right mind to make any more of my position at the bistro. This change to start over might spark something new, something different and good. Mostly I came home because you have cancer and need support. Mom, you were always there for me, now let me be there for you."

"I'm the mother. Of course, I was there for you. But you're supposed to be out living your life, having babies, buying a home, and becoming a world-famous pastry chef."

Chloe scoffed. "Well, life saw fit to do otherwise and there is no place I'd rather be. Fame, ah, it'll wait for me." She glanced toward the photo booth strip she'd taken with Sam Hardy. "I bet if you ask him, fame is way overrated anyway."

Mom turned away, brushing the back of her hand over her cheeks. "All this mush is making me hungry. I'll get my pocketbook and we can go."

"Sounds good." Chloe reached for her handmade leather bucket bag she and Jean-Marc had found at a custom shop in the

French countryside, and her favorite beret. She looked again at the boxes. Tomorrow. She would unpack tomorrow. If she'd learned anything from death, it was to not worry over the small things.

"Does Ella's still have fabulous milk shakes?" Chloe followed Mom down the stairs.

"You bet." At the coat rack, Mom and Chloe pulled on their winter coats before stepping into the Tennessee cold. "Let's walk. Ella's isn't far."

Their brisk walk was under a blue winter sky laced with the gold, red, and orange of the setting sun. Each step brought memories of running and playing down this lane with her friends. Riding her bike in the summer and throwing snowballs at the neighbor boy, Landon Martin, in the winter. She'd read in the latest Rock Mill High alumni newsletter he was a Wall Street mover and shaker now.

"Hearts Bend was a great place to grow up, Mom." Chloe slipped her arm through her mother's. "I have so many good memories."

"I'm glad. Hearts Bend is a great little town."

They turned off Red Oak Lane and headed down First Avenue. Across the way, Gardenia Park slept under a blanket of old snow. Mom's breath billowed about her head as she chattered and pointed out the new ice-cream flavors Pop's Yer Uncle Ice Cream Shop advertised in the window—Peppermint and Vanilla Sweetheart—as well as the pretty twinkle lights glowing inside Valentino's restaurant, the donut and muffin-shaped paper cutouts on the plate glass window, along with a placard propped on the sill of Haven's Bakery. Oh, she had a million memories of Saturday mornings at Haven's with Mom.

The more they walked, the more Chloe's memories surfaced, and she was awash with sentimentality. By the time they entered Ella's, she almost believed coming home was just the tonic she needed to shoo away the rags of death. Here she could ground herself in the truths that raised her.

Tina, Ella's pretty and peppy owner, approached with two menus and surprise in her eyes. "Chloe! My goodness, the famous French pastry chef graces my humble diner." Tina's hug felt like a warm drink on a cold, blustery day.

"Stop, I'm not famous. Not even close." Chloe slid into the second booth from the door and glanced out over Gardenia Circle, the park, and the slotted parking spaces filling up with folks coming to dine after a long workday. "But I do owe you for letting me bake and sell MeMaw's vanilla cake here. Remember that?"

"I sure do. Even back then you were a whiz in the kitchen. And darling, 'round here, anyone who makes it as the pastry chef in a Michelin-starred Paris restaurant is a big whomping deal." Tina handed Chloe and then Mom a menu. "Meredith, how you feeling? I've been praying for you."

"I'm fine, but I'll take all the prayers I can get."

"I'll be back with some waters, then y'all can order." Tina propped her hand on her hip. "Welcome home, Chloe."

The simple sentiment hit Chloe in the chest and her eyes flooded. Mom stretched her hands across the table and squeezed Chloe's arm but, like the wise woman she was, said nothing. Chloe reached for a tissue in her bag as Mom saw a couple across the way and went over to say hi, which led to her talking to the couple in another booth and the big, long table of what looked like town council members.

Look at you, Mom. She looked more like a council candidate than a woman battling a cancer diagnosis. But Chloe had seen the mammogram, read the biopsy report, talked to the oncologist while she was still in Paris.

"Fast growing, but caught early"—thank You, God—*"very treatable."*

So. Mom had cancer. People survived cancer all the time. Still, the thought stabbed icy fear into Chloe's heart. She took a deep breath and smiled as Mom's laugh echoed around the diner. She would be okay. She had to be.

Chloe dug in her bag for another tissue. Instead of the soft-pack that had taken up a recent permanent residence in there, her fingers brushed a stiff piece of paper, down at the bottom, wedged into the corner seam. With a gentle tug, it came free, and she smoothed it open on the table.

Oh my. She'd forgotten she'd stuck that list in her purse. How many months ago? Well over a year, it had to be. Our Goals for the Year, written in her neat script.

Jean-Marc's list focused on business: *Convince Papa to hire a social media manager. Research and contract with new microfiber vendor.* Hers covered both her job and her marriage: *Institute mentoring/coaching at restaurant. Weekly dates. Save 20% of our income for the café.*

A tear landed on the page, smudging the percentage sign. She remembered now. She had put the list in her purse to have it laminated, so it wouldn't curl and fade when she taped it to their bathroom mirror. But she'd forgotten about it. And then every time she had made a savings deposit, the balance was less than the last time. By the time she'd figured out Jean-Marc was making withdrawals, she'd been about to open a separate account to save for the café.

She crumpled up the list and stuffed it back into her bag as the waitress, Spicy, brought two glasses of water to the table. Chloe ordered a burger, fries, and a chocolate shake. Mom hurried over to say she'd have the same.

When Spicy left, Mom squared off with Chloe, that *mother* look in her eye. "You always tried to take care of me. It was cute when you were ten and endearing when you were sixteen. But now you're thirty and I do need some support. I admit it. We will get through this together, but darling daughter, I can't have you hovering and worrying. You'll drive me bonkers. So, here's an idea." Mom drew a deep breath and gave Chloe a tremulous smile. "Why don't you get a job?"

TITANS NEED A NEW FRANCHISE QB. ONE WITH TWO WORKING KNEES. @SAMHARDYQB15'S CAREER SEEMS TO BE FADING ALONG WITH HIS KNEES. SAVE THE $$ AND GIVE IT TO SOMEONE WHO CAN BRING HOME THE RING. #DUMP-SAMHARDY

— @NO.1 TITANFAN ON TWITTER

ACKNOWLEDGMENTS

From Mandy:

This has been a wild ride, and there are so many people to thank. It takes a multitude to complete a project like this.

Rachel Hauck, thank you for selecting me to participate in this process. Without you, this book would not be what it is.

To the team at Sunrise Publishing, Susan May Warren, Lindsay Harrel, Rel Mollet, Kate Angelo, Barbara Curtis, and Katie Donovan—thank you for all the time and effort you poured into getting this novel out there. Y'all are amazing.

My Hearts Bend sisters, Carrie Padgett, Carrie Vinnedge, and Carrie Weston, thank you for your support, your friendship, your prayers and encouragement. Now we can shimmy, right?

I wouldn't have finished this process without the support of my friend Tari Faris. Thank you for your hours of listening, encouragement, prayers and support.

The teaching at My Book Therapy has been outstanding, and the support system they've created is amazing. Thank you to my huddle buddies: Tammy, Jennifer, Sarah, Renee, Tari,

Gracie, Rachel, Heidi, and Deanna. Thank you for those hour-long calls and all the prayer. And to my friends, Andrea, Alena, Jeanne, Kariss, Lisa, Michelle, and Tracy. Thanks for believing in me.

For the always full cup of coffee that has seen me through this process, I have Angela, Trevor, Kiefer, and Hannah at JoJo's Coffee and Goodness to thank. Keeping my cup full kept me going.

Obviously, I wouldn't have finished this process without the love and support of my real-life hero. Thank you, Sam, for always letting me follow harebrained ideas. For supporting me as I wonder what I've gotten myself into and encouraging me to seek God when I am overwhelmed. Stella and Johanna, thank you for letting mommy follow this dream and talk to imaginary people and for laughing at my stories when I needed a pick-me-up.

And Mom, Dad, and Julie, thank you for being the listening ear—my support—and for telling me I'm doing okay, even when I know I'm not. Thanks for making dinner, picking up kids and groceries, and acting as my very own laundry fairy.

I saved the most important for last. I had no idea the lessons I'd learn through this process, and I wouldn't have completed it without the overwhelming graciousness of my God. He is always good.

And a note from Rachel:
Thank you, Mandy, for all your hard work!

ABOUT THE AUTHORS

New York Times, USA Today & Wall Street Journal Bestselling author **Rachel Hauck** writes from sunny central Florida. A RITA finalist and winner of Romantic Times Inspirational Novel of the Year, and Career Achievement Award, she writes vivid characters dealing with real life issues. Readers have fallen in love with the quaint and loveable small town of Hearts Bend, TN introduced in the NYT bestselling *The Wedding Dress,* which launched her Wedding Collection novels. Visit her at www.rachelhauck.com.

When **Mandy Boerma** isn't hanging out at her favorite coffee shop writing, she's a busy mom. After meeting Prince Charming, they started their own version of Happily Ever in the Florida Panhandle. Nothing compares to life at the beach. While those early days included romantic sunset walks with sand between our toes, days are now filled with sandcastles, swimming and school. Mom-duties fill Mandy's days. You know them all—cooking, cleaning, chauffeuring, organizing, helping at school, all the lessons and practices, homework, etc. And because that's not enough, she also teaches piano, normally with coffee in hand. Visit her at www.mandyboerma.com.

You'll Be Mine: A Hearts Bend Novel

Published by Sunrise Media Group LLC

Copyright 2022 © Sunrise Media Group LLC

For more information about Rachel Hauck and Mandy Boerma, please access the authors' websites at the following respective addresses: www. rachelhauck.com and www.mandyboerma.com.

Published in the United States of America.

Cover Design: Jenny at Seedlings Designs

Illustrated Map: Brenda at Penmagic Designs